John Kitchen

Mine-Shift

europe books

www.europebooks.co.uk | info@europebooks.co.uk

ISBN 9791256970995

First edition: April 2025

Mine-Shift

Other books for older children by John Kitchen

Nicola's Ghost

A Spectre in the Stones

Jax' House

*The Rainbow Talisman (*Co-author George Acquah-Hayford)

For younger children

Kamazu's Big Swing Band

For older readers

Fragments of Springtime

This book is dedicated to whoever reads and enjoys it

and to all those who love and cherish books

My thanks go to members of Oxford Writers' Group and Ann Granger for their constant advice and support.

Also to Stephanie Hale whose tireless help and encouragement was incremental in forging every link in the telling of this story.

To Dr Steve Lacey whose knowledge of medical treatments was invaluable in the writing of this book.

And to Lauren, Veronica and the team at Europe Books without whom this book may never have seen the light of day.

Chapter 1

He was running through a mist, dodging frantically between the yellow flowers of gorse and the lace edged May. Ahead of him a white hare loped, veering left and right, while at his back he heard pounding feet. He knew what was following. His pursuer was a black mastiff dog, and in his head voices screamed of carnage and destruction.

The dog was gaining now. He could feel its breath hot on his back. Then the ground gave way and he was falling – down, down, and deeper down to the bowels of the earth. He was in a mine – not the mine where he worked. This mine was lit in a strange way, with a steady, unnatural light.

All around him there was chaos. Water cascaded in from the sea. Broken pieces of the mine's ruins floated by, and there were bodies – shiny faced boys lying face up, arms and legs spread. He grabbed at one hoping to save him from drowning. Then he let the creature go. It wasn't human. The shape was human, but its flesh was cold, formed of wax. All the bodies appeared to be effigies floating helplessly, nudging each other like boats in a storm.

Pushing through the water, he ran. Behind him now he heard the ringing bark of the black dog again. It echoed through the shafts and levels until, in some weird transformation, it began sounding his name, "Joel, Joel." The barks reverberated in his head. Then… "Come on, Joel, boy." He was being shaken, and the sound had changed to his mother's voice. "Joel. Come on, boy."

Slowly he looked around.

His mother was leaning over him, her hands gripping his arm. Behind her he could see the anxious face of his younger brother, Obadiah, peering over her shoulder. He pushed himself so he was standing, and he stared. The peats in the fire were glowing, with traces of smoke curling to the chimney, while the trivet straddling the peats carried a steaming kettle. There was a wooden table and scattered, roughly hewn chairs. In the flickering of the tallow candle, he could see the pallet where his mother and father slept, but today nothing seemed real. A few seconds ago he'd been looking at the strange, floating effigies, the weird level with its unnatural light. And he'd seen the white hare and the black mastiff dog.

What he'd been looking at had blocked out the room, even though he'd been awake. It was as if he was seeing a vision. It scared him. He knew what the hare and the dog meant. Running together they foretold the most terrible of disasters. His father had told him only a week ago about Zeph Hosking, a fisherman down at St Ives. He'd seen the hare and the dog. Yet he'd insisted on taking his boat out. From nowhere a storm had blown up. The boat had been smashed to pieces up by Hell's Mouth. Not one of the crew had survived, and there were other stories, scores of them, where the sighting of the white hare running with the black dog had foreshadowed catastrophe.

His mother was shaking him again, slapping his cheeks, because he was still in the trance. "It was like you was in a faint, boy. You wouldn't come to, and your eyes was wide open. Your father's gone to the mine. He couldn't afford to stay, but I never knowed you out like that. You wasn't here with us."

He shook himself, still unsure of reality. "I'm all right, mother," he said. Then he went to the table, scooping cold water from a bowl, dousing his face and shocking himself back to the present.

His mother grabbed his croust bag. She slipped it onto his shoulder. "Here," she said. "Now you'm back with us again you best get over to the mine. Cap'm Bolitho won't put up with no lateness. Your pasty's in your bag, so get out there, quick."

He shuddered as he adjusted the croust bag and closed the cottage door. A mist had rolled in off the sea. The whole moors were blanketed in an opaque darkness, with barely a sound except for the whisper of air off the downs. But he breathed deeply. Even the dank of a Cornish autumn was a relief after what he'd seen.

Then, as he stumbled over the broken barrier to the next field, a tingling dread danced on his skin. Coming from behind him was a rustling, as if a spirit was parting the grasses. He didn't have time to turn either, before he saw what it was, and seeing it made him stagger to a halt. Shooting past him, ghostly, almost as if the fine droplets had sucked themselves into an animal form, was the white hare he'd seen in his trance, darting and zigzagging, its ears thrown back. Now there was the other sound, stronger, more urgent. His instincts told him not to look. But he had no choice as, lurching through the grass in pursuit, he watched the black dog, muscular, with slavering jaws and limbs flying.

He couldn't move. It was as if he was still locked in the trance – as if his mother, Obadiah, and the cottage room he'd just left were all part of the dreadful vision… Yet, the feel of the mist, the penetrating wetness of autumn that soaked into his shoes and britches, that mist and that wetness were real. The darkness draping the downs, the air that moved on his face, they were in the real world. He hurried through the field again, listening to the whisper of his feet through the grass… What he'd just seen wasn't part of any vision. The hare and the dog that had passed him a moment ago were real-life omens of disaster, and his father and the others were already preparing to go down the mine.

He broke into a run. He had to warn them, but it would be hard. Even to mention the white hare and the black dog threatened bad luck.

As he stumbled on across the fields the outlines of hedges and cottages loomed. There were shadowy figures, cloaked in the fog, moving towards the mine. He could hear the chatter of men assembling at the pithead, along with the rumble of the pump and the engine house with its great beam engine, booming and hissing. He could see the mist, yellowed with smoke and flames, as the shape of the mine buildings glimmered through the fog.

Quickly he scrambled into his mining smock, leaving his britches and shirt in a neat pile. Then he shuffled through the slow-moving queue until he reached his father.

"What happened to you then, boy?" his father snapped.

"I don't know, Father. It was like I was in a trance. I couldn't free myself." He pushed closer and spoke in a low voice. "But Father, you know that thing what you told us about Zeph Hosking?"

His father nodded. "Tragic story. Don't go talking about it here though."

"But you got to hear me out, Father. On the downs when I left home, I seen it – the white hare and the black dog. It wasn't part of no trance neither. They was both there in the mist, and they was real."

His father's lips tightened. "Not here, boy. Tell me later, back home."

Several of the others clicked their tongues. A couple swore under their breath, aiming kicks at him. "Hush your noise," one of them said. "Careless talk. We don't want none of that."

"But Zeph Hosking… and all them other things what have happened," Joel said. "You got to listen to me."

They were moving towards the shaft now, and his father snapped, "Just hold your tongue, boy."

It was what he'd feared. As they went into the pit it felt as though the men were clambering towards some kind of calamity. Worse, he was going with them, down to the confines of the rock face, where there'd be a disaster – and there was nothing he could do to stop it.

The miners peeled away as they climbed down, some heading off at the first level, some at the second. All the time the heat grew, and the spaces became more enclosed. They clambered from wooden ladder to wooden ladder as the shaft followed the seams of ore. Eventually, they reached the third level where he and his father worked. By now the heat was stifling. The air felt heavy with the rancid smell of sea-salt, the reek of old stone and the floor's saturated wetness. But hovering over it all was the sickly-sweet stench of gunpowder. It was this gunpowder that was used to blow open the gangue where the seams of ore were, and it was the smell of it that made Joel shudder. Today, setting gunpowder in shot-holes was the task of his father's team, and he knew it was the gunpowder that was likely to trigger the disaster.

Candles spluttered reluctantly. Sometimes the air was so putrid it could hardly support the flames. Then one of the boys would be told to sit over the candles, fanning them back to life so the men could see to work. But today the flickering light was just enough. He watched his father take the tapers one at a time, setting them in balls of clay, pushing the clay into the floor so that they stood free. Finally he handed one to Joel. “Set this up there by the face, boy,” he said.

Joel’s own job didn’t require much exertion, but it did need courage. He had to hold a bar to the rock face while the others hit it with heavy mallets. A jumping bar they called it. All the time, as the blows rained down, he had to turn it, screwing it into the rock. He knew he mustn’t flinch. One false blow and his fist would be shattered. It had happened to another boy. Now his hand was nothing but a useless pulp of smashed and fused bones.

The men teased him as they worked. “That Joel Penberthy, Billy,” someone said. “I heard tell he been seeing your daughter. Did you know that? Hand in hand up round the back of Tehidy, so I heard.” All the time the blows thudded down, sending ringing reverberations into the pit, shuddering against his grip. “Think we should teach him a lesson, do you? Give that hand a bit of a tap so he won’t be so keen to grab your girl’s hand no more?” The men laughed and winked; even his father laughed. Joel knew his face was on fire.

“It could easily be done, boy,” Billy Jewell said. “Ain’t you scared, holding that bar?”

He was scared. He was always scared. But it wouldn’t do to let the men know. “That’s all right, Mr Jewell,” he said. “I know your aim is good, and you know I never took your daughter around the back of Tehidy.”

It was the truth. In fact he’d never taken anyone’s daughter anywhere – even though other boys of his age were married; but that was another thing he wouldn’t want to share with the men.

All morning the heat grew, and the sett became more airless. They were gouging out a series of shot-holes. This afternoon they would clean the holes, dry them with clay, then set the gunpowder and fuses, and all the time Joel's thoughts hovered around the white hare and the black dog. It was as if fate hung, waiting for the moment when the fuses were lit... and then… what?

At croust time they took a break.

The miners ate together, often up at the second level where the air was less stale. But Joel hardly ever sat with the rest. He felt uncomfortable with the banter and the teasing. It was known he kept himself to himself. He would wander off with his croust and find some place alone, where he could be with his thoughts – let his imagination roam free.

He didn't go far. He could still see the yellow glimmer of light where the others ate. He could still hear their raucous laughter.

Today he was particularly careful eating through his pasty. He needed to make a special effort to appease the knockers. The old ones had told him that little men inhabited the mine – Bucca, they called themselves. They were reckoned to be the souls of those who'd crucified Jesus. They'd been cursed to live in the mines for eternity. If you kept on the right side of them they were good creatures, but they were very bad if you didn't treat them right. Every day the knockers demanded their morsel – their didjan – from the miners' croust, and every miner would leave them the crust of his pasty. No one doubted that, if you cheated the Bucca and ate the crust, you would take ill and die.

He clutched the crimped crust as he ate so he wouldn't touch a crumb of it. Then he laid it beside him, still with some potato and gravy clinging to it. When he'd done he whispered: "I left you some extra didjan, Bucca, so keep us safe tonight."

Then he collected his croust bag, making his way back to the others. He kept his eye on the flickering glow of their candle. But, as he groped against the walls, the light seemed to change. It became more a white haze – and steadier. It struck him as odd. He felt that he was climbing. The smell had changed too. There was a hint of clean saltiness, and the air had a greater age to it, as if the passage he groped along was ancient. He was aware of rubble and rock falls lying in his way. Sometimes he had to clamber over great piles of boulders.

He wasn't in the level any more. Behind him the darkness had thickened, with no hint of candlelight from where his fellow workers should have been – no sound of laughter. The whole place seemed gripped in a silence that was near death – as if all his workmates were gone, swallowed into an eternity, and he was the only one who remained with any kind of a living heartbeat. It frightened him. He'd never been in such a place.

He knew he was lost. He must have wandered into an uncharted shaft, or part of a disused stope, one of the large caves the miners dug to extract a seam of ore. He had no idea where he was, but pressing on had to be the best choice. He could feel the waft of fresh air on his face. If the stope led to ground level there would be landmarks he'd recognise. He'd be able to find his way back to the pithead. If he found that, he could go down the main shaft again and get back to his father.

He struggled over the heaps of broken earth and stones, scratching his arms and legs on sharp granite edges, slipping on loose shale, until, breathing heavily, he came to the surface. But as he emerged he stared around him, stunned. Nothing was right. A white mist still drove in from the sea. It had a different smell though. This morning the mist had been heavy with the flames of furnaces and the reek of smoke. There'd been the sweeter smell of hot oil from the steam pump. Now the air was clean, fresher than he was used to.

Then, as he looked around, his blood ran cold.

Surrounding him, glimmering through the mist, were the gorse bushes he'd seen in his vision, in full yellow bloom, while the trees – the hawthorn trees – were white with May.

Nothing made sense, and he staggered, collapsing helplessly onto a grassy bank.

Chapter 2

For a few minutes he didn't move.

How could time have shifted like this? Was it the work of the knockers? Had they pushed time forward to next spring so he would be completely clear of whatever was going to happen in the mine – or had they pushed time back?

He looked at his arms and hands, dusted by rock fragments, then at his feet and shoes. Everything looked much as it had when he'd set out for work. There was no half-year of growth, nor was there a half year of shrinkage. He knew he'd had a big growth-spurt through the summer. He didn't seem to have lost any of that.

Standing, he stared around him. But there was no comfort in what he saw. He seemed to be in a world that had shifted away from everything he knew.

He began to walk slowly down the hill. The sky was lighter in one direction, as if the sun was trying to break through. If he followed in that direction, it might lead him back to the pithead.

As he carried on walking though, shapes loomed further down the hill, shadowy – but clear enough for him to make them out. It looked as if there was a street down there – something like the streets in Redruth and Penzance, with a row of houses. But... they weren't like the houses he knew. These houses were neater, with well-built walls and evenly tiled roofs. Some were two storeys high like those in the posh parts of Redruth; others were lower, single-storey buildings, although they weren't rough cottages like his father's. For a moment he hardly dared move, but the full intensity of what he saw hadn't yet dawned. Curiosity made him draw closer. As he did, he could make things out more clearly. The doors of these houses were well fitted. So were the windows. They had panes of glass that were large and clear, rooftops edged on the ridges with neat red stonework. The slates were blueish-grey, cleanly cut.

Each cottage had its own garden, something like those he'd heard about in posh places – the Basset's in Tehidy, or those gardens at Godolphin Manor – places his father had talked about. But this was in a different world from the one he'd woken to this morning. A path ran between the two nearest cottages. It wasn't a mud pathway though, or even grass. It was smooth, with a hard, blackish-blue surface, better than any road he'd ever seen, better, even, than the turnpike road down to Penzance. Almost in a dream, he followed the path towards the fronts of the houses where he saw a wider road – like a highway, made of the same black-grey material. But there were no ruts or gaping potholes. The road had a kind of edged walkway, and it was far wider than the toll road to Penzance – with white dashes and lines marking its centre. It was easily big enough for two carts to pass each other.

He stood at the walkway's edge, full of a dizzy fear and curiosity. Then he heard a noise that made him throw himself against the hedge. He saw an enormous cart. There weren't any horses, yet this thing was moving, and its speed was terrifying. In less time than a blink it shot past. Behind it were carriages, brightly coloured, with clear glass windows. These carriages were shaped in a way he'd never seen before. Each one dashed by at speeds that left him petrified. None of them had horses to drive them. He thought he glimpsed people inside – like himself – yet not like himself. Sometimes there was just one, sometimes more. He couldn't tell what made them different, because they shot by at such speeds, but now he knew, this place and these people weren't like anything in his world. The knockers hadn't transported him away from danger. This place, the place with the flowering gorse of his vision... it was hell – or heaven – or... his brain couldn't begin to grasp where he might be. All he knew was, with those monstrous things tearing past, it was a place of great danger.

In panic he turned, racing back up the hill. At least the grass and downs up here, the shrubs and trees, were similar to those he'd seen in his own world. Gasping for breath, he sat on the grassy outcrop, his heart pounding. He had no idea what to do or where to go.

But then something appeared out of the mist. It was like the things in the carriages – in some way human. Fear made him want to run, although this creature was slim and looked very capable of chasing him.

It had the features and limbs of a human, wearing the tightest of britches, black, clinging to its legs right down to its calves, and it had shoes that were pink and white. They were made of fabric instead of leather. It wore a kind of shirt, like a blue, tight-fitting smock – with a white bar across the chest. With britches like this it was certainly wearing a man's clothes. The hair was cut short, brown and neat, as a boy might have it. But what confused him was the shape around its hips and chest. They were not boy shaped. Yet they weren't really girl shaped either.

In desperation he struggled, remembering things the pastor had said. He remembered him telling them that the angels in heaven were like this – neither man nor woman. He'd said they didn't marry, nor were they given in marriage. This creature fitted that description, neither boy nor girl. He was wondering if he'd died and this was an angel, although it didn't have the wings he'd seen in stained glass windows in Illogan church, but by now the creature had come near enough to speak. He heard a light voice say, "Hi. I haven't seen you around before."

Some of the words it spoke were the type of words Joel would use, but its accent seemed odd. It looked at him hard, as if it was puzzled. The thing was attached to a small dog with short legs and a squashed face. All it said was: "I'll take Shelly off her lead and let her have a run." It leaned forward, unclipping the dog so that it bounded up the hill. "Not too far, Shelly!" it shouted. After that it looked at Joel again and smiled. "She's not really mine. I'm walking her for a neighbour."

This slight creature did seem friendly, and some of his terror abated. That wasn't the only thing that impressed him either. As it sat beside him on the grass bank, he could smell something unlike anything he'd ever smelt coming from a human; something beautiful and fresh – the perfume of the most wonderfully scented flowers. When it moved it filled the air with fragrance, swamping his senses. Having this creature so close gave him the same feeling he sometimes felt for Rose, his older brother's wife, and the smell made him feel it even more. He was beginning to wonder if he was wrong about this being an angel.

There was no time to think about that though, because the creature was looking at him again, out of large, brown eyes. "You're not local, are you?" it said. "Not from around here?"

"I don't know no more," he said. He had to make an effort to speak. "It be all different from when I went down the pit this morning. When I come up out of that stope, croust time, I... well, I don't know where I am."

What he heard next didn't make any sense at all. "You've come up from the mine?" the thing said. "You must work for my dad. Are you an actor? He told me he was getting actors dressed up as mine workers – you know – as guides for when he opens the mine to tourists."

"Your dad?" he repeated, struggling. "He do own the mine?"

"Yeah. Do you work for him?"

"If he own the mine, I do," Joel said, but this mine wasn't the mine where he worked, and this place... "Working for your father, though – here – that don't seem right to me."

As he spoke the thing brushed an arm against him. The arm felt warm and soft, as if it was flesh and blood. He knew from the pastor that this wasn't how an angel's arm should feel. But, if this wasn't an angel, it must be human – a boy – a beautiful boy, but certainly a boy.

"I'm Cass Blake," the boy said. "What's your name?"

"Joel Penberthy," he replied.

"That's a Cornish name," said the boy. "You must be from around here."

"Cornwall be where I grew up," Joel said. "But this place – them buildings down there – that ain't nothing like the Cornwall I do know."

"Down Polgwenvor, you mean?" the Cass boy said. He was looking at Joel again, with the same quizzical frown Joel had noticed when he first arrived. "But, come on, stop messing me around. You're an actor working for my dad, yeah?"

Every word seemed wrong. It was nonsense. Joel wondered whether he'd fallen asleep over his croust and was dreaming. "No," he said. "I ain't no actor. I'm Joel Penberthy, son of Amos. We work down the mine. My father and my older brother, Habakkuk, and his wife, Rose. She'm a bal maiden. I help my father. This morning we was drilling shot-holes in a new gangue, ready to blow open the seam.”

The boy’s look seemed to be piercing right through him. “How old are you?” he said.

“Fifteen – sixteen next January. I been working down the mine since I was twelve.”

“You’ve got to be joking,” the boy said. Then he did something that froze Joel. He leaned over, with those smells from the hedgerows full of perfumed flowers, and he flicked Joel’s hair. He said, very softly, in a way that brought a sweat out in Joel: “With hair like that you’ve got to be an actor. It’s great, that hair. You’re dead good-looking, you know that, don’t you?”

What he’d done, flicking Joel’s hair – and the words he’d spoken – that wasn’t natural. Joel felt he had to say something. “If you’m a boy,” he croaked. “– It don’t seem right – to touch my hair and talk like you’m doing.”

Then the boy laughed. “You’re kidding. I’m Cass – I told you – Cassandra. You know very well that’s a girl’s name. You know exactly what I am.”

“But...” he said. “You’m wearing britches, and that hair, it be cut short like a boy do wear it, and you ain’t buxom, not like the bal maidens and other maids what I know.”

By this time the thing began to look uneasy. “Give over,” it said. “You know this is what girls wear. I mean...”

Then it asked the strangest question. It was frowning, still looking puzzled. “Who do you think is our – like – ruler; you know – on the British throne?”

“Well, that be George of course. King George the third. Everybody know that.”

He saw the thing open its eyes and stare. “Nobody’s going to believe this,” it said. “And I know you’re trying to make me look stupid. I mean, you're telling me you went down the mine in Georgian times this morning, and came up here, over two hundred years later, at lunch time?"

Everything around Joel swam – so much so that this thing that now claimed to be a girl had to put an arm out to hold him steady. "Are you OK?" it asked.

He shuddered. "I don't understand the words you'm saying. You'm saying this is Cornwall, just the same as what it was when I woke up this morning, but since I went down the pit two hundred years have gone?"

The girl laughed. "Well, it would have, if you really were from the eighteenth century."

She was still holding him, because he'd lost all sense of balance.

She was gazing into his face. Having her so close was making his heart race.

There was a small scar on his cheek, just under his left eye – where a shard of granite had flown up when they were drilling shot-holes. She brushed it gently, while her face coloured. She looked at his hair again. It was hanging loose and straight, falling to his shoulders, shining the colour of chestnuts. "You've got the looks of some guy out of Drama School," she said, "– and that hair – it's like, you could be in a boy band."

He'd never met someone as forward as this – but everything here was so different. It was hard for him to grasp what she'd told him. All he said was: "If you'm a maid, no maid should do them things, nor say what you'm saying."

She smiled uneasily, but her brown eyes glinted. She was so different – so – un-girl-like, and yet she was beautiful. "Yeah, actor boy," she said. "We women – we're liberated – and you're winding me up."

At last he stood. “I don’t understand,” he said. “And how did I get here? You tell me that.”

The girl, Cass, stood up too. She was almost as tall as he was. Her movement set loose even more of those perfumes. As they walked towards the stope the dog emerged from behind a gorse bush. “Well,” she said. “I guess you’ll be telling me you came through a portal, is that what’s coming next? – Some door in the mine – an entrance to a time warp, yeah? You’ll try and con me into believing there’s one in the shaft, is that it?”

He wrestled to get hold of what she was saying. He thought he understood the idea of a door. He’d noticed something change as he tried to make his way back to the others, when the light moved from a flickering candle to that silvery stillness. He looked around. From the road he could still hear the roaring of those machines.

“I don’t belong here,” he said suddenly.

“What do you mean, you don’t belong?” she demanded.

“I don’t fit.” He turned towards the stope. All of a sudden he was desperate for an escape. “Do you think, if I went back down there, I could get to my own time again, where I belong? I need to be back so I can help my father. We got to set the gunpowder in the shot-holes to blow open the seam.”

“OK,” she said. “You could give it a go, but you can’t pull anything over on me, Joel Penberthy – or whatever your name is. You won’t get anywhere. You’ll have to come out again – and I’ll wait. I haven’t got anything better to do this afternoon.”

He still didn’t understand, but this place – it was so wrong, so impossible. He wanted to get back to his father, even though that meant he might have to face some sort of disaster this afternoon.

Suddenly, without thinking, he said, "I got a mind there'll be an accident in the mine where I do work this afternoon, but, if God spare me and I ever come back, would you be here?"

She smiled. "You bet. Like I said, I'll wait your return with baited breath – and it'll be about ten minutes, that's what I reckon."

He began to walk cautiously into the gaping cave, pushing between the growth of gorse. He could still see this girl; she was standing at the mouth of the stope, tall in her strange, skin-tight britches, with the dog sniffing around her heels.

Then he forced his feet to walk into the void, and as the darkness closed in, one thing stayed with him; the image of Cass. Even though the world he was running from scared him, if he survived the afternoon, something made him want to find this stope again.

It would mean getting back to the Cass girl, and he was keen to do that.

Chapter 3

To begin with, the grey light of the twenty-first century shone from the entrance, showing some kind of route, but as Joel went further, darkness swallowed him. The musty earth and the ancient stones began to breathe into his lungs. He could feel the skeins of cobwebs, hung like foetid fabric from the walls. It took him a long time, groping, struggling over obstacles. Suddenly he began to panic – not just because of the stifling grip of age and decay, nor because of the small chasms he had to work his way through, but because, now, when he turned, the strange white glow he'd followed earlier wasn't there. There was no sign of Cass's world... nor of his own.

He stopped. He was lost, just as he had been when he'd found the stope at croust time. He tried to grasp what Cass had said. Suppose her 'door' had closed – shut him off from her world, yet denied him entry to his own?

But he had to get back. He had to believe – even if all this was totally unbelievable – if he climbed upwards there would be an entrance to the new world, and unless the way was completely blocked, downwards would lead him to other tunnels and he'd be in his own time again.

Breathing heavily, he carried on into the stope...

There wasn't any dramatic sensation that heralded something like a door in time – nothing to announce he was back. It was just the levelling out of the floor – and a familiar atmosphere of a mine that felt like Gwenvor. There were distant sounds of picks and mallets, the voices of miners back at their work, and he stood with his heart thumping.

His legs were weak from the shock of what had happened. He had to grip the wall for support.

Things only came into focus gradually.

He had no idea how long he'd been away, but he knew there'd be trouble when he found his father. As boys brushed past him there were comments. Some shouted, "Where you been then, Joel Penberthy? You'm late." Others sneered: "What you been up to? Your father, he'm jumping mad down there."

His father and the other men were fiddling with shot-holes, drying them with clay, but there were more to be drilled.

"I got lost, father," he said, running up. The air had worsened and running made him breathless. Someone had been set to fan the candles. "I went up a stope what I never seen before. I couldn't get back."

His father pushed him roughly. "You deserve a hammering, boy, going off like that. We'm all behind now. Why can't you be like them other boys – eat your croust along with us?"

Billy Jewell pushed the jumping bar into his hand. "Never mind that now, Amos. He'm back. We just got to catch up on lost time, that's all."

Through the afternoon the blows rained down. Joel concentrated on swivelling the bar. He couldn't allow himself to think of Cass or the weird world he'd been to – or the white hare and the black dog. He didn't think of the hare and the dog at all; not until the shot-holes had been drilled and dried out ready for the gunpowder.

It was always his father's job to push the gunpowder into the holes. It had to be done well, with just the right amount of powder. But, today, Father was riled. Joel watched nervously. He seemed to be going too quickly.

"Father," he whispered, kneeling beside him. "I know I shouldn't have got lost. That was wrong. But it don't do to let your anger take hold. You'm going too fast. You'm putting in too much powder."

His father didn't look up. "I been doing this since before you was born, boy. And I wouldn't be going too fast if you hadn't gone off on some fool's errand, croust time, making us all behind. Out of my way. Leave me to get this finished."

Billy Jewell was behind him. "Do what he do say Joel. He know what he'm doing. You come up here with me."

Joel stood back, uncertain. It was as if, suddenly, he understood why he'd been chosen to see the dog and the hare. If something did go wrong, it was him, Joel Penberthy, who was responsible. This speed of his father, the anger that was burning in his soul, was all of Joel's making.

The shift was coming to an end and his father still hadn't finished. The mine-employed workers, the tut workers, had already gone to the shaft. The others, the tributors, always worked on until the blast, because they were paid by the amount of ore they won. Every second worked was precious.

For Joel, now, it was a matter of waiting – until his father said, "Done!" He held out a hand, adding: "Now, boy, that candle, give it here. Then head for the carts."

There were several of the team with tallow candles poised over fuses, ready to light them.

Then it happened, with a speed that didn't leave a second for any thought except self-preservation. Joel's father shouted, "Trucks," and from all down the level, men ran. They made it for about a hundred yards, dodging through the twisted confines of the level, to where there were carts standing.

Joel ran so he could get as far from the smouldering fuses as he could. He and the other boys were younger and smaller. They ran more quickly, but only as far as they dared – to the count of about thirty. After that they had to take shelter.

They darted behind a truck and at last the sound of footsteps died.

The stillness was thick with tension. It could only have been for two or three seconds, but it seemed an age. Joel closed his eyes, bracing himself. Then there was a heavy boom. A rush of hot, sulphurous air shot down the level, rushing past them – it was like sheltering in a gun barrel. He heard the boom ricochet to the far end. Then the air was sucked back – an eerie wind against their backs, while they stayed, crouching, waiting for the shock to die.

Normally, after the explosion, there were a few seconds of silence followed by the excited chatter of men and boys as they came out from their hiding places; but, today, as the rumbling faded, there was a new sound – splitting rocks – cries from farther down the level – a ground-shaking cascade of boulders. Candles went out and the place was filled with a pandemonium of darkness.

Joel leapt from behind the truck, choking as the debris rose. "My God!" he gasped. "Them rocks. They've comed down!"

All along the level came cries and shouts from the men. For a moment he couldn't speak. This was the work of the hare and the dog. But he knew there were able-bodied boys sheltering with him. The men down further needed every hand to help them.

"Is any of you hurt?" he called.

The boys were still cowering. A few whispered, "I don't think so, Joel."

"Well, come out. We got to get down there, see what's happened, do what we can to help, because some of them men is in a bad way."

Someone shouted, "Can somebody find a candle and flint? Give us a bit of light so we can see what we're about."

There was scrabbling and a few sparks. Orange-yellow flames began to flicker, and Joel gripped the truck, gasping.

He could see great boulders and rocks lying in pools of water. Trucks lay on their sides, smashed to splinters. Bodies were spread across the floor, with limbs moving in the carnage. There were groans and curses as the pain kicked in.

A couple of the younger boys were crying. He put an arm around one. "Hush," he said. "It ain't no good crying or being scared. We ain't hurt. It's them up there what's hurt. We got to think about them."

Up at grass level they would know about the rock fall. Someone would be tolling the mine bell. Men would be on their way with planks of wood to carry the injured. The bal maidens and women from nearby cottages would be assembling to look after the wounded. All Joel and the boys could do as they made their way towards the wreckage was hope that the exit to the shaft hadn't been blocked.

Billy Jewell was standing near him. He was holding a tallow candle which he handed to Joel. "Here, boy, you'm smaller than me. Take this and get in there, see what's in that pile of rubble."

Joel called to one of the older boys and they began to roll the rocks away, freeing a pathway to a splintered truck. The other boy went ahead as, all down the level, men and boys struggled with fallen debris, moving broken bodies into the main thoroughfare.

The boy with Joel tore desperately at a lump of granite until it shifted. But then he shouted: "Joel, come here, quick. I think I got your father."

A flash of grey hit Joel's eyes. It was as if, for a second, his mind had died. Then came desperation and an uncontrollable drive. He didn't know what gave him the strength, but he shifted the granite rock with one push, kneeling down, directing the candle.

His father was lying with his face twisted in pain. He was trying to speak, but Joel touched his lips. "Hush, Father. Save your strength. We got you. We'll get you out."

As he spoke, his father's head fell back and his eyes closed, while Joel looked him over in the spasmodic candlelight. But when the light shone on his right leg, he almost fainted. The leg was buckled below the knee, twisted into a grotesque shape. Where the boulder had struck there was a gash of a wound. Blood was congealing, while sticking out from the wound was the splintered end of a broken bone.

He looked at his father's face again. "It be all right, Father," he whispered. "We got to move you. It's going to hurt, because your leg been hit, but we'll do it quick."

He nodded to the other boy – then, holding him as gently as they could, they pulled him away from the rubble.

By now men had made it from grass. They were loading the injured onto boards, moving them to a wagon at the end of the level. There they would be winched to the surface. Others, with fresh candles, were searching the fallen rocks.

"Is that Amos?" one of them said.

"My father, yes," said Joel. He was shaking. "You get him out safe. He'm a good man."

But his father still had his eyes shut. He didn't move as they took him to the cart.

For a while the men carried on searching. Joel and the rest of the boys stayed back. They had to, in case smaller bodies were needed to get into narrow fissures. Eventually, though, it was clear there were no injured men left. Fourteen had been carried to the shaft on boards – men who he and his father knew well – men who his family called friends. Later, when they'd come to grass, he found that two of those who'd been injured had died.

He was one of the last to leave, but as he climbed onto the ladder, from deep in the mine's belly, he heard another rumble, followed by a tumultuous sound of water, like falls and rapids, and he knew the walls had ruptured. The sea was running in.

There was chaos at the surface – men wandering around aimlessly, or sitting nursing small injuries. Some had been blinded by dust, while others struggled for breath with dust gone to their lungs. The bal maidens and other women were washing wounds and eyes, but it was the sight of those lying prone on the boards, motionless or groaning, that hit at Joel. Two thoughts filled his head. One of those prone men was his father; and he knew, all this chaos and carnage was his fault.

A tut worker who'd been helping with the wounded brushed past him.

"Have you seen Father?" Joel called.

The man pointed towards the dressing floor. "Over there. Your brother, Hab, he'm with him, and Rose."

"Tell the Cap'm I heard the walls breach," Joel added. "There be water running in from the sea."

He found his father lying on a board, with Hab and Rose tending him. Now Father's eyes were open, although, somehow, Joel wished they weren't. They said the eyes were windows to the soul... and his father's eyes reflected nothing but pain.

"How is he? How's Father?" he said.

Hab didn't look up. He could see they'd tried to put the leg back together. They'd found an old smock. His brother was ripping strips to bind the wound. But there was no love lost between Joel and Hab. Hab wouldn't show any patience. His only response was: "Place is like a battlefield isn't it, boy? And word has it, it's all down to you, coming back late, holding up work, making Father rush with the powder."

Joel saw his brother's black hair, matted against his forehead. His dark eyes would be smouldering. Hab had always been hard on Joel. People said that Joel had the brains in the family – and he knew he didn't have Hab's manly stature. Somehow he felt this was what his brother held against him.

"I got lost," he said. "I couldn't help it, Hab. I couldn't find my way back. I did tell Father to be careful."

But Hab just turned and spat on the grass.

"Leave him be," Rose said. "The men down level three told me he done wonders rescuing Father. Billy Jewell said the boy saved his life."

Hab still didn't look up. His voice was stiff with rage and he snapped, "Well... whichever ways you do look at it, he'll have done something. If father do live, he'll have saved his life. If he die, the runt will have killed him, and that'll be the bare facts of it."

Rose put an arm around him. "Take no notice, boy. You just leave your father with me. Go down the engine pool, have a good wash and get dressed. Then the two of you will have to carry Father home on that board. It won't be no easy job neither."

He tried to whisper his thanks, but the words were choked. Hab was right. If his father died, it was his fault. He'd have killed him as surely as if he'd put a pistol to his head.

Chapter 4

By the time Joel had washed and put his shirt and britches on, Hab had bound Father's leg. But nothing had changed in his mood. "You got the strength for this have you, boy?" he growled. "Because I can find a proper man if you ain't up to it. Then you can walk along with the maids."

"He'm my father, Hab," Joel said. "I shifted the rock what crushed his leg, and I can bear him home." He picked up the end of the plank, struggling to match Hab's movements, but the plank made a dead weight. "You watch him, Rose," he whispered. "Hold him steady, so he don't fall."

The journey was going to be long. Every time Joel's arm gave, his father let out a groan.

"Will you be careful with that board, boy?" Hab snarled. "Every jolt do hurt Father. Can't you see that?"

"I'm doing my best, Hab," he said. He tightened his grip, measuring his tread. "Only, it be hard to keep hold."

"You ain't thinking straight," his brother snapped. He was leading up a hill now, and because Joel was at the back and was smaller, the board sloped steeply.

"Lift your end up, for the love of God," Hab growled. "You'm going to have Father in a heap on the floor before you'm finished. You'm always somewhere else, in some dream or other – coming back late. Don't you forget, it was you what caused all this, because you can be certain, I shan't."

"It was the knockers," Joel said. "They led me into this stope what I never seen before."

But that only made Hab's shoulders stiffen. "You'll find any excuse. It won't never be Joel Penberthy, the boy what's too stupid to find his way around a pit level. The boy what's got his head stuck so far into the clouds, he can't tell night from day."

As they struggle on, the weight set a pain gnawing in Joel's arms making him ache all along his spine. Rose touched his arm gently. It was a comfort in a harsh world. He peered at her through the darkness. He could picture her. Her brown eyes were like Cass's eyes, but her face was round and her skin more ruddy from the weather. Her dark hair fell around her cheeks in a halo of curls. She was more the way of the girls in his own time, in touch with the earth, with the downs and the dank of Cornish mists. "You stop tormenting the boy," she said. "You'm always laying into him."

He heard Hab swear under his breath, while every lurch made his father groan. He seemed to be getting weaker. Rose shook him. "Stay with us, Father. We ain't far from home now."

It was well into the night, though, by the time they reached the cottage.

His mother was waiting with Martha Curnow, a near neighbour. Martha had brought news of the disaster.

There was fresh straw laid on the pallet. Someone had spread a cloth over it. Pieces of wood glowed in the grate along with the peat. Soup was steaming in a cauldron.

It was a rough and ready place, not like the houses of Cass's time.

"Is he hurt bad?" his mother said. She had her hands thrust into her apron, gazing anxiously into his father's face. The single tallow candle hardly gave enough light to show the twisted limb. Joel hoped she'd be spared the sight of the wound and the splintered bone. Hab had done a good job binding the leg, although there was still a disfiguring distortion in the way it lay. His mother would see that.

Obadiah came out from a corner, crying.

"We wasn't sure if your father was still alive," Martha said. "When my Robert come back from the pit, he didn't know. They was saying some of the men had died."

"Father's all right," said Hab. He looked sharply at Joel, as if he wanted to say more, but Rose managed to speak first.

"Thanks to Joel, here," she said. "He found him and freed him from the rocks. Billy Jewell said it was him what saved his life."

His mother glanced at him and nodded. "He'm a good boy."

"He ain't that good," Hab growled. "If he hadn't come back late from croust, none of this would have happened."

"Never mind all that now," said Martha. She was busy with the cover on the pallet. "The important thing is to get your father onto the bed and settled."

"And hush your noise," Joel's mother said, giving Obadiah's arm a slap. "Father's all right. He'm back safe and sound. That snivelling isn't going to help nobody."

But Martha was looking at Joel's father anxiously. "You should get a doctor out to him, or a surgeon, Sarah. He don't look good to me."

"Doctors and surgeons wouldn't do nothing," his mother said. "They'd only bleed him, or saw that leg off. And we haven't got no money for doctors nor surgeons."

As they lifted Father onto the pallet, though, the stress of carrying him was bringing Joel to breaking point. He felt his legs buckle, while the heat from the peat and the smell of the soup and straw – the airlessness and the fumes – made his vision swim. Suddenly he staggered. "Hab, he'm right," he said. His voice was shaking. "I made father rush. The gunpowder wasn't loaded proper."

"You don't know that," said his mother. "Father's good at his work. He wouldn't have done nothing wrong setting up they shot-holes. It ain't the first time a level have come in."

"But he is right, Mother," Joel said again. "It were my fault."

Rose whispered, "Hush, boy. It been bad for you – the accident, rescuing Father, carrying him all that way." She looked at Hab. "He do need a drop down the ale house. You let him go with you tonight, and don't you be hard on him. He ain't much more than a boy, and he'm your brother."

Hab didn't want to take him, Joel knew that. He'd be at him as soon as they were outside, but, once he'd got a few pints down him none of that would matter.

They were heading for a particular ale house that he liked. It was on the fringe of Redruth. It had a kayle running down the side; a low shed where the men played skittles for a gallon of beer. But what Joel liked was; this ale house had two books displayed on the mantel – *The Book of Common Prayer,* and *Robinson Crusoe.*

There weren't many books around. Most people couldn't read: but Joel could read. The pastor had singled him out when he was young. Every Sunday, after church, he'd gone back to the pastor's, learning to decipher the words of God's book from Genesis right through. But the Bible was the only book he'd ever read. Even when the pastor wanted him to read in church – which he did on special saints' days and at Christmas – he was only allowed to read out of the Bible. He wasn't even allowed to read from the Prayer Book. Joel had often looked longingly at the two books in the ale house, wishing he could get his hands on *Robinson Crusoe,* so he could read something that wasn't God's word.

It was partly the fact that the pastor had taught him to read that caused the rift between him and Hab. As they trod the downs, the silence was grim, with just the occasional grunt from his brother. The only noise was the chatter and the tell-tale clank of tankards, which they could hear long before they reached the ale house.

Because of the accident the miners had flocked for the beer. It was their only escape from the harshness of death and injury. Inside, the air was thick, with men crowded to the door. Hab pushed through, gripping Joel by the shoulder, ordering his usual – beer, laced with brandy – for them both. Then he took the tankards, steering Joel through towards the kayle.

It was less crowded there – colder and not so chaotic. Men had gathered by the walls, making room for an alley so they could bowl. Through the game they chalked up signs on a board to identify themselves. They kept a tally of chalk strokes to show their score. But, tonight Hab wanted to exploit Joel's talent. He shoved him. "Go on, boy. You'm so clever. You spell out 'Hab' and 'Joel' on that board. Show this lot what you can do."

Joel knew what Hab was doing. He wanted to draw out hostility from the men, but a lot of those who were playing went to the church in Illogan. They knew Joel could read – and when he scrawled the two names, there were grunts of approval. One of the older ones called across, "He'm smart, Hab. He do form they words as good as you'd see in a book." Then he said, "Do you do numbers, too, boy? Think you could stay there by the board and keep count of all the scores, do you?"

The guilt of causing the accident made Joel content to accommodate the men, and they played on into the night, going back to the ale house in steady drifts to collect more beer – with the occasional drink for Joel, because he was keeping the tally; but his head was beginning to swim.

Men called across to each other about this one or that, injuries to heads and arms and legs, and as the drink loosened tongues the fate of the injured men grew worse. They would all certainly die unless the Good Lord intervened with a miracle.

It was the mention of miracles that made a little man called Sam Eustice shout, "That's what we do need, ain't it? – a miracle to save our boys. We need to get God on our side." He glanced across at Joel and added, "There be a prayer book in there on the shelf, Joel, boy, ain't that right? Do you think you could read out of that prayer book for us? You know – read like you done in church – a prayer to the Lord God Almighty, so He do look down on us in His mercy and save them poor souls what was hurt up the mine today?"

Part of Joel's brain told him that, by this time, he could hardly mark up the tally. The board seemed to be lurching around, and the marks were blurred. The whole kayle was careering around. He knew it was the drink. But the brandy that laced his beer was giving him a new belief in himself. It felt right – a chance to make amends for causing the disaster. "If that be what you want, I could try," he said.

Immediately they staggered back to the ale house, shoving until the men were packed shoulder to shoulder. Sam had hold of Joel's arm. He steered him across to a chair by the mantel. "Stand up there, boy," he said. Then he grabbed one of the books and turned, shouting, "You men. Let's have some hush in here." He had a powerful voice for a small man. "We been talking out the kayle. Our people be dying all around us, and we'm needing a miracle."

Someone shouted, "Amen, brother."

"And that's what we'm getting," Sam said. "We'm going to get Joel Penberthy, here, to read out of the prayer book, like an oblation to the Lord, so He do look down on our men and bring them back to health."

There were a few murmurs of, "Here, here." One man shouted, "He could do it. He do read the scriptures for us in church."

Joel was struggling to stand steady on the chair. The grey swamp of faces seemed to be reeling all around him, and balancing was hard; but at last Sam opened the book and thrust it into his hand, hissing, "Here, boy. Read down from the top of that page." After that he turned to the others again, staggering slightly. "Could we have the reverence of the church in here, do you think? Like as if the pastor himself was here. Hold our heads low, bowed to the Almighty."

Joel looked at the page and squinted. Then he cleared his throat. One of the men shouted, "Come on, boy, we'm all ready." But the two candles in the house hardly gave any light. The words were difficult to make out. They seemed to be moving, as if they were sliding off the page.

He cleared his throat for a second time, and at last he began. "*I looked,*" he read. His voice sounded louder than he'd expected. "*And saw.*"

There was a cry from the mass of bowed heads, "Amen to that," while more called, "Yes, Amen, brothers."

"*And saw...*" Joel struggled with the words. "*Plainly the place where they had been.*"

"That be right," Sam Eustice shouted. "He would. The good Lord do see everything."

There were yet more grunts and slurred "Amens." But the words refused to stay still on the page. The whole room was revolving around. Every time Joel looked, the letters started their steady slide.

"*But no appearance of them,*" he read.

It was impossible to string a meaning together, although Sam understood. "No appearance of them," he shouted. "The Almighty, the invisible God. Read on, boy, read on."

He struggled with the words until, at last, he read: "*but having now more courage... and... consequently, more curiosity, I take my man Friday with me...*" And straight away there was a yell from Nicholas Williams, the landlord.

"Man Friday?" he shouted. "What's the boy doing? He'm reading the wrong book. That be *Robinson Crusoe.*"

In an instant Sam Eustice grabbed his arm, hissing, "Here, boy, what you playing at? You give me that book."

Just below him, Joel saw Hab with a face blazing in fury. "You done it now, runt," he shouted. "You'm the stupidest fool on God's Earth. You put a curse on all of them sick men. Father will die. They'm all going to die, cursed because of your blasphemy."

The rest of the men were yelling too, almost spitting with rage. "You heard what Hab said. Our men be cursed. The Lord have been insulted here tonight."

He didn't know what to do, but then a hand gripped his arm, easing him off the chair. It was Billy Jewell. "Come on, boy," he said. "It wasn't your fault. Anyone could see that. It was that damned fool Sam Eustice. You come with me. I'll take you out the back, out of harm's way."

He led Joel through a door into the now deserted kayle, then into the calm of the fog-blanketed moors, but Joel was stunned.

“I don’t know what I done, Mr Jewell,” he whispered. “Hab said I brought a curse on all they sick men – I didn’t know it was *Robinson Crusoe* what I was reading.”

“No. ‘Course you didn’t. It be Sam Eustice. He’m all mouth and no brain. He’ve always been like it.” Billy glanced back at the ale house. They could still hear the roars of outrage. “It’ll take a few days of sober thought for this lot to die down,” he added. “Best you come home with me. Lie low for a bit.”

But, back at the cottage, Joel had a father who’d been injured in a disaster that was his fault. Now, according to Hab, Father was cursed to die because of his blasphemy. “I got to go back,” he said. “Father and Mother, they do need me, and the boy, Obadiah.”

“Do you think you’d be able to make it across to Father’s on your own,” Billy asked. “Or shall I come with you?”

Joel peered into the fog-wrapped darkness. “I done that journey before,” he said. “I can get home all right.”

“I’ll go back to the ale house, then,” said Billy. “See if I can talk some sense into they drunkards.”

He made his way back, while Joel watched, before turning slowly towards the moors.

Chapter 5

Even when he'd moved away, the cries sounded in his head.

He heard his voice pronouncing the words; "Consequently more curiosity – I take my man Friday with me," – then there was the shout from Nicholas Williams.

And it *was* blasphemy to read out of *Robinson Crusoe*. It would have insulted God beyond forgiveness, and with the brandy in him, he couldn't see anything but his own guilt. He'd stood on the chair. He'd read out the words. He'd fooled the men so they believed he was reading from the prayer book. Somewhere in the back of his head he knew Sam Eustice had given him the book, but Sam couldn't read. Joel should have known it was the wrong book.

He felt sick with shame, but, slowly, he made his way across broken walls and rutted fields until, up ahead, he saw a window with the faint yellow smudge of a burning taper flickering behind the glass.

Rose was sat near the fire, beside Mother, feeding the flames with peat turfs. She looked up when he came in. "Where's Hab?" she said.

He was still unsteady, and the fumes and heat made him stagger. He leaned against the door, glancing at the unmoving shape on the pallet. "He'm still at the ale house. I comed back on my own. How's Father?"

"He ain't too good," his mother said. "He'm sleeping, but he've been proper restless all evening."

His father was lying on his back. Even in the weak candlelight Joel could see his face, pale and grey. There was a sheen of moisture – drops of sweat running from his forehead, cold and clammy.

"Haven't you got no rug to cover him?" he asked. "He'm as cold as a fish."

"There'm a rug in the basket," said his mother. "We'm doing our best, keeping the room warm. He took a drop of soup just now."

Joel laid the rug across his father, stroking his forehead.

"Why have Hab stayed down that ale house?" Rose said suddenly. "Why, with his father sick, ain't he back here with you?"

He sat on a stool, clasping his hands, staring down, watching his fingers twine around each other. He didn't know how he was going to tell them. At last he said, "I done something real bad down the ale house, Mother. I think I made certain Father and all they others will die. They was all shouting when I come away. It was Billy Jewell what got me out."

His mother stared. "Whatever did you do, boy? What would you have done to bring about your father's death?"

"I brought down a curse," he said. He could hardly get the words out, he was so ashamed.

"Who told you that?" said Rose. "It ain't in you to do no curses, especially on your own father who you do love."

"It wasn't done deliberate, Rose. It was Sam Eustice what had the idea."

His mother snorted. "Sam Eustice. Say no more, boy. That man's brain is in his mouth, always have been. He'm as stupid as any man I know."

"But the idea was good, Mother. It was me what ruined it. Sam wanted me to read a prayer out of the prayer book, only I read out of *Robinson Crusoe* by mistake."

"Couldn't you tell the difference?" said Rose.

"I had so much drink in me I could hardly make out the words, but Sam, he was making it out like it was a prayer. All the men was shouting 'Amen' and 'Hallelujah'."

His mother sniffed again. "All so soused in beer and brandy they would have said 'Amen' to a receipt for Saffron Cake. I could never see the merit in downing liquor like it was water."

"When I read out the words 'man Friday', Nicholas Williams saw what I was doing. Then they all turned on me. They said I'd insulted God. Hab said I brought the curse of death on all they injured men."

"Was it you what fetched the book?" his mother said.

"No. Sam Eustice gave it me."

She got up and went across to the bed, wiping his father's face with a cloth. "Well, it be Sam Eustice what's at fault then. There ain't no blame can be laid on you, boy." But she sighed. "All the same, it be a bad thing to be praying to the Lord using a heathen book." She settled by the fire again. "I don't know what will come of it."

"I'm sure the Good Lord will understand," Rose said. "You can't take no blame, Joel. The men will see sense when they'm sober. And I can't believe God Almighty would take the lives of innocent men just for one mistake."

But his mother didn't look convinced. "Some of them stories what the pastor do give us, Rose – the Lord is a mighty jealous God – but it wasn't your fault, boy."

It was no comfort to him though. His mother was right. It wasn't God's practice to be easy on mistakes, and whatever she and Rose said, he was the one who'd read out the words. He was the one who'd called down the curse, even if he didn't mean to.

At last Rose stood up. "Father look to be settled for the night," she said. "Hab won't come back here when he'm done. You got Joel now, Mother. I'll be making my way. You know what Hab is like. If I ain't there for when he turn up, he'll make trouble."

She and his mother walked to the door, letting the chill blow across the room. It made Joel shudder. He took his father's hand. "I ain't going to let you die, Father," he whispered. "I brought they rocks in on you like I'd pushed them myself. Now I took God's help away, but I ain't going to let you die."

By now his mother was standing behind him, with the door closed. "No, you won't," she said. "You'm a good boy to him. You always have been. Now go over there with Obadiah and get some sleep in."

He looked at her, standing there, stout as a rock, with her hair black, streaked with grey, pulled back from her face. It was a stern face, lined with hardship, but it was his mother's face. Gently, he kissed her on the forehead. "Thank you, Mother. You know I'll do everything to save Father. He ain't going to die."

"No," she said. "He ain't. Now you get some sleep. I'll sit up with him tonight."

Obadiah was curled at the back of the room. Joel moved to let the warmth of his brother's body creep into his chilled clothes. Then, slowly, with the heat and airlessness of the burning peats, he fell into a restless sleep. But he was haunted by memories; of falling rocks and splintered bones; while words tumbled in his head. 'I looked… and saw' – And cries of 'Amen' mingled with shouts of 'Blasphemy'. He could see wide, black roads, with horseless machines roaring past. There were neat low cottages; and Cass's face, smiling at him, with the smell of flowers – and the sickly stench of gunpowder, together with roars of explosions and rushing water as the sea broke through to the third level.

When he woke, the room was in darkness. He fumbled for a candle. His mother was sitting on her chair by the pallet, her head drooping forward. There was no movement from the pallet, but Joel could see the film of sweat on his father's face. He ran a hand across his forehead. Now it was hot and sticky, as though he was burning up.

He touched his mother's arm and she sprang up. "What's going on?" she demanded. "Is Father all right?"

"He'm asleep. But he'm hot," he said. "Like he've been took with the fever." He put the candle in a holder. "We got to wipe him down. I'll wet a cloth – try to take some of that heat out of him. Then I got to go to the pit."

His mother turned stiffly, resting her hand on Father's face. She nodded. "He is too hot, Joel, boy. You get water, but I'm thinking you shouldn't go down that pit today. They men at the ale house, they'm harbouring a grudge."

"I got to face them, Mother," he said. "I can't hide for the rest of my life."

She sniffed. "Nothing but drunken fools, led by that dolt Sam Eustice. You'm worth a thousand of them, boy. If they hold this against you, it be wrong. It be Sam Eustice what gived you the book, and I'll warrant he was running his mouth all the time you was reading."

"You're telling it like you was there, Mother," he said.

She gave another contemptuous snort. "I know Sam Eustice. And if you go down the mine, don't let Hab bait you. He's jealous of your brains, and though he'm my son, I got to say, he've got a nasty streak in him."

"I'll be all right," he said. "You just look after Father till I get home. I'll sit up with him tonight."

He could see hints of dawn by the time he reached the mine. The buildings were outlined, spectral and grey, but today the sight disturbed him. The hiss and boom of the engine seemed wrong, along with the yellow touches of flame and smoke from the stacks. The crippled mine should have been silent, grieving for its injured and dead; but that wasn't the way of the world. The business of winning ore from the earth was the only thing that mattered.

Men and bal maidens were lost as to what to do, stunned with the shock of disaster. He eased his way through, but the news wasn't good. The badly injured hadn't shown any signs of getting better. He picked up snatches of conversation about sweating and fever. His name was mentioned, along with fragments about prayer books and curses. No-one went out of their way to speak to him.

Hab and Rose were with a group by the dressing floor. Quietly he joined its edge, awkward and uncertain. For a few minutes they carried on without realising he was there. But Rose had seen him.

"How's Father?" she said.

"Much the same. He got the fever. Mother sat up with him."

One of the men looked across. "It be a bad business, boy, these men sick, and now, what with the evil eye put on them..."

"It is," he said. He couldn't pretend it wasn't. "It be a bad business all round."

Hab glared at him. “Well. What you planning to do about it? You read out of the book. It was you what put the eye on all our men.”

“But Sam Eustice gave him the book, Hab. He only did what he was told,” said Rose.

“It was him what done the reading.”

Someone said: “The only way to be rid of that evil eye is to bring in the Pellar.”

Immediately Hab turned to Joel, “Rachel Pengelly, down Newlyn. The white witch,” he said. “They say she can do cures and lift the evil eye. What about it, boy. You ain’t man enough for that are you? Not to go down Newlyn and fetch Rachel Pengelly up here?”

But it was a way out – something he could do to help with the guilt. “I am, Hab,” he said. “I’ll go tomorrow – on the Van. I’ll gladly bring the Pellar back.”

There were approving grunts. He hoped the news would get through to the others; but it would be a slow process. The rest of the day stretched out long and harsh.

The pumps and winches were working, but, with the mine flooded, there was no direction. No-one could go down the pit without being told what to do, and none of the mine captains were there. It was a tense wait until Walter Bolitho called them to the pithead.

The pumps had been working at full capacity, he told them, but the third level hadn’t cleared. The breach was too big. Now all the underground men were to spend the day sealing the level. It had to be closed and new excavations made. He said bal maidens and grass level workers should continue dressing and vanning the ore as usual.

The men working underground had to take rubble from the slag heaps. It had to be shovelled into the flood waters until the whole third level was sealed.

All morning Joel sweated with the kibbles of slag, groping for ladders. When the men settled at the second level for croust, he slipped away again. He could still see the flickering light from the candles and hear the murmur of voices, but there wasn't any raucous laughter today; just the menace of muttered words. After a while he began to feel the isolation. What if the men were talking about him? He would be better sitting with them so he could defend himself and remind them that, tomorrow, he was going to fetch the Pellar.

He put his part-nibbled pasty into his croust bag, feeling his way towards the candlelight.

But, once again, as he groped, the ground under his feet felt strange. He sensed he was climbing. All around, the air was changing, getting cooler, with that clearer, fresher feel.

The glow ahead of him transformed from a flickering yellow to a white, steady lustre. There was the uncanny feeling that his workmates had been left back in another age – that all life but his had gone... And he knew he was climbing towards the new world – to Cass, and those horseless machines with their crazy speeds, and the smooth tar-blackened roads.

Chapter 6

It was a very different day when he emerged.

The sky was brittle blue, flecked with white clouds, and the sun was bright. As he sat on the tuft of grass he had to shade his eyes. Now, with the mist cleared, everything took his breath away. He recognised familiar landmarks. To his left was the hill he knew to be Carn Brae. Down below lay a rash of woodland, something like Tehidy – it was where Tehidy had always been, but now whole areas had been scattered with houses and other buildings. He could make out roads running between the hedges. Strange carriages crept by, and beyond the fields the sea spread, a deep blue and glinting. He could see boats with no sails – although the boats seemed to be moving freely across the bay.

He didn't know how he felt. If he had been here in his own time, apart from the sheep and cattle wandering, there would have been nothing. Now there was constant movement.

Then something made him shrink back. It was a low growling, coming from the sky, and hovering into view from behind the hills, he saw a monster, hanging in the air like an enormous insect. It gave him a powerful urge to run, but he didn't. Instead he sat, watching, as the thing nosed across the bay.

At last its ferocious growling faded into the hum of the other machines and it disappeared.

If only Cass was here to explain. He looked hopefully to catch sight of her, but all he could see were the rolling browns and greens of the downs, and the scatterings of gorse and May. Eventually he got up, wandering towards the houses, the place she'd called Polgwenvor.

Today the flowers around the houses seemed brighter. He noticed a sort of bed set up on the grass in one of the gardens – cleverly fashioned, with straps across it. He would have liked that for his father. It would be more comfortable than the straw and the pallet.

He knew he mustn't stay too long; although, with all the confusion in the mine, if he did get back late, it wouldn't be difficult to rejoin the others.

He made his way down the path between the houses, careful to make sure no-one saw him. There were many more carriages today. Some were small, with the odd shapes. They seemed to pass very quickly. He could see the humans inside. But there were carts that were bigger and slower, more box-like. As they rumbled past, the ground shook, making him cower against the hedge.

It was clear, on the smooth surface of the road, these monsters knew where they were going. None of them veered into another one's path, even though there were carriages and boxes moving in both directions. They seemed to have an assigned section of road, those travelling left from where he was crouched, on his side of the road, while those travelling to the right kept faithfully to the other side.

Every now and again one of the smaller carriages would be followed by a bigger thing, another box-like structure. It seemed that the box-like thing was being towed, as if it was a carriage being pulled by a horse. These things were often some shade of white, but they had windows and a door, almost like small cottages on wheels. There was so much to take in. He was beginning to be less frightened.

Then a woman approached. She was pushing a little carriage along the walkway, with a baby in it. There were two small girls beside her, dressed brightly, holding onto a bar on the carriage, prancing beside it. But the woman was heading towards him.

He knew he didn't fit, so, deftly, he slipped down the path, back up to the moors, hoping he hadn't been seen.

He was desperate for Cass to be waiting, but the hill was still deserted.

He had to admit though, he was becoming more curious about this world. He glanced towards the woods of Tehidy. There was a clear route down the field. He could get there without having to go near Polgwenvor. Down there he would have more space to watch what was going on, and he'd be hidden by trees. It would also give him time, in case Cass came. From the woods he'd be able to see her on the hill.

He made his way to the woodland's edge, where a path dropped to the valley, falling to a cluster of white houses. This path was more like those in his own time, just rough stone and grass. He walked down it, ready to slip behind a tree if any other human appeared. At the bottom he could hide and watch unseen.

But when he reached the valley, something made his head spin. Spread out on the hill to his right, rising back towards the summit was a whole village. It wasn't like any other village. The dwellings were smaller, and it looked as if they were constructed of cloth; green, orange, brightly coloured, all set up in their own grass patches. Some of the patches had carriages standing by the dwellings – like the ones he'd seen on the road. On other patches there were those box cottages on wheels. Then there was an area where children were playing on frames, with a few stone-built buildings scattered among the cloth dwellings.

People were sitting outside on their grass patches and he was amazed; these places were even more simple than his father's cottage, yet the people who lived in them seemed so content. Some read books or large sheets of paper. It looked as if everyone could read. They had beakers, resting on flimsy tables. Occasionally they leaned across to sip from the beakers. A few cooked on devices set up on the grass, or on low tables, and the air was filled with the most mouth-watering smells. It was a world away from what he'd seen earlier, almost like a settlement of tinkers and gypsy folk, although these people weren't like the travellers of his own time.

He was so captivated he didn't notice a boy coming down the path until it was too late.

The boy was about his age, wearing black britches that clung tightly to his legs, hardly reaching his knees. He wore a thin fabric top, white, without sleeves. His hair was short, very fair, with a hint of curls, while his smooth face was bronzed. He carried a kind of board under his arm, and he was smiling. Joel began to wonder why he was so afraid of these people. They all seemed friendly. The boy greeted him much as Cass had. "Hi," he said, but Joel wasn't confident to reply.

"Is this where you do live?" he said at last.

The boy adjusted his grip on the white board. "Yeah. Me and my family, we're on holiday. We've been surfing down at Portreath, but the waves aren't up. Besides, there's this book I wanted to finish. Do you live around here?"

There were words in what the boy said that Joel didn't understand. 'Surfing'. He had no idea what that meant, and 'holiday' – he knew of Holy days, but how could a person be 'on holy day'? It seemed the boy hadn't noticed his dust and grime, or the smock – or else he was too well bred to make a comment. He didn't want to say anything that would betray himself, so all he said was, "Yes, I do live up over that hill – a few miles off."

"We're down from London," the boy said. "Usually we go to Newquay, but the surf's great in Portreath." Then he put the white board across to his other arm and added, "Are you into surfing?"

Joel shook his head. He wasn't sure how the question had been put together, but he guessed what the boy was asking. "No," he said. "I don't do that."

"I'd be down on that beach every day if I lived here," said the boy.

By now his words were becoming more mystifying. But, this place, where people lay out in the sun, sipping drinks, reading books by their cloth dwellings, this place where they went to the beach with white boards, this village seemed to have no cares – and that was something he liked very much. "I got to work," he said. "And I don't have no beach near me what I could get to."

"Shame," the boy said. "And if you live here all the time, I guess you'd take things like surfing and all the holiday stuff for granted."

This was another string of words that left him baffled. He was beginning to feel uneasy.

Suddenly the boy said, "I'm going up to our site. You could come up for a coke if you felt like it."

He sensed the invitation might be dangerous though. He understood very little that the boy said. Joel didn't know what a coke was, and he was afraid he'd say something that would betray him. "I got to get back, working," he said. "But you'm proper kind to ask me."

"No sweat," said the boy. "Another time, perhaps. We're here for a fortnight. What's your name?"

Joel told him, and the boy said, "I'm Ewan. Ewan Anderson." Then he added, "Come back another day if you're around. We could have that coke, or we could head down to the beach. I'll get you body-surfing on my board."

He patted the white thing under his arm.

"If I can, I'd like that," Joel said.

"We're at the top of the field – site T eight. It'll be no sweat finding it." He turned for the settlement. "I'll get a shower then, and finish that book. Don't work too hard."

"I won't, not if no-one do catch me," said Joel.

As he made his way into the cloth village, the boy, Ewan, called over his shoulder, "See you later."

But Joel was still confused. 'Get a shower'? A shower was rain. Surely that wasn't something you could get as though you were fetching it from a shelf? It was a strange world. There was danger from the fast-moving things on the road – yet, the way these people lived, warm, with no tension, in the fabric village… something about this second visit fascinated him.

He made his way back through the woods, up towards the hill. Then he remembered his pasty. It was still in his croust bag – he'd hardly eaten any of it. Now, in the bright sunlight, he felt hungry. He thought he would finish it here – it would give him more time, more chance for Cass to come. But as he was eating, he noticed something glinting in a fissure of rock by the stope's entrance. It was some sort of glass container, wedged into the rock. A bag of some kind was sticking out of it, and there were objects in the bag – a folded piece of paper with words on; then, what looked like a modern version of the pastor's pen. As he pulled the container out, unfolding the paper, another stiffer square of paper fell to the ground. Hurriedly he retrieved it, staring at it in amazement. What he was holding was a 'likeness' – so perfect that only the cleverest artist could have painted it. It had a smooth surface that shone, and… it was a picture of Cass's face, with her smile and her glinting brown eyes. He guessed Cass had written the words on the folded paper too, so he moved into the brighter sunlight, where he could pour over the writing.

Some of the words were unfamiliar. They certainly couldn't be found in the Bible, but the pastor had taught him how to combine letters to sound out new words. He'd heard some of them from Cass's lips, too.

"Hi Joel," he read.

A thrill shuddered through him. The 'likeness' and this letter had been put there for him.

"Came up here with Shelly this morning hoping to see you, but you weren't around. I've left this, hoping you'll come back sometime and find it. If you do, please write. You can do it on the other side of this letter. Put your note in the plastic bag, and then put it back in the bottle. I've left a pen for you. I will come every day at lunchtime, and guess what? I'm writing this because I'm starting to believe what you told me – I mean, how crazy is that? But I waited outside the shaft for ages yesterday and you didn't show, so I looked inside. There wasn't any sign of you. There was no other way out of the shaft either. You seemed to have disappeared off the face of the Earth. So, and I know it's mad, but I'm starting to think you actually did come through a time warp.

Keep the photo. It's for you, and please, please, please come back and write on this note!

"Love or whatever,

Cass x"

He worked out the words he didn't know. He guessed the container was the bottle. She'd said the 'likeness' was a photo. It was his to keep. He tucked it into his croust bag, settling on the outcrop to answer her message. There was a point at the end of the pen, and even though there wasn't any ink, when he dragged the point across the paper, it left a mark.

He was slow forming each letter. The pastor hadn't spent much time teaching him to write. He was more concerned that he could read. But he could form the alphabet. A word was just a series of letters taken from the alphabet.

Where he could, he used the same words and phrases as Cass.

"Hi Cass," he wrote, copying the greeting from her letter. *"Came here hoping to see you."* Then he stopped. He would have to make some words because they weren't in Cass's letter. *"I did not find you,"* he wrote. *"But I will come back."* He thought for a moment. He wanted to say he couldn't come for a day or two because he had to go to Newlyn to fetch the Pellar, but he couldn't form those words.

He took the pen again and wrote: *"I will be back in two days or three at croust time if I am spared."* He'd taken a long time, and he'd nearly filled the page. He copied her greeting.

"Love or whatever,
Joel x"

After that he took the paper, along with the pen, slipping them into the bottle, and he returned the bottle to the fissure.

Chapter 7

It wasn't hard to slip back to work. He found a kibble that he heaved to the next drop. But there was a grimness, with men and boys shouldering past, muttering whenever they saw him. Later, at grass level, Rose was with Hab – but Obadiah was there too.

Rose called him over. "Mother do want us home," she said. "Father's took worse."

That scared him. "Should I go now, down Newlyn, to fetch the Pellar?" he asked.

"It ain't no good doing that," said Hab. "There won't be no Van leaving for Penzance, not till first thing tomorrow."

"What's wrong with Father?"

"He've got all hot," Obadiah said. "And he shout out, like his head ain't right, saying things what don't make no sense, and he do throw his arms around, sweating like a pig."

Suddenly an urgency eclipsed Cass's world and the pain of the afternoon's struggles. He didn't know what he would do when he got home, but he had to do something.

Hab muttered, "Pity we haven't got the Good Lord with us. We could have done with Him at a time like this."

When they arrived, his mother was beside herself. "All day he've been like it. He ain't right," she said.

His father was wet with sweat. His mouth was dry and his lips cracked. Mother had been feeding the fire, and the room was choked with heat and peat fumes. "Haven't we got no water?" said Joel. "And a cloth. And Mother, we do need spare clothes for him. What he'm wearing is soaked, and that ain't good." He began to undo his father's shirt. "It's the heat in his body what's making him bad. We got to take that away, and his lips, they'm cracked with dryness."

Obadiah fetched a beaker to wet his father's lips, while Hab got water and a cloth. "Then find something to make more strips, Hab, while I look at that leg," he said. He glanced at Rose. "You stay with me, Rose."

In all his life he'd never issued instructions like this, but a need to save his father was driving him. Even Hab followed his directions.

Joel tore the wet clothes away, then began to wipe his father's face and body.

"Wet his lips," he whispered. "And let him have water – in sips – so he don't take too much."

But when he saw the wound, his stomach lurched. It was like a slab of meat, festered with yellowing pus. It was congealed with blood and the smell was rank. "I got to wash this," he whispered. "I got to get that filth out of him."

He worked on, re-binding the leg, drying the sweat from his father's body. With his mother's help he got him into fresh clothes while Rose kept feeding him water.

Slowly he saw the stress fade. For a minute Father opened his eyes before he sank back onto the pallet.

"You done a good job, boy," Rose whispered. "You fought for your father's life here tonight."

"Thank God," said his mother. "I thought, this afternoon, we'd lost him."

Obadiah was crying again, but his mother turned to him with: "It don't do no good crying like that. Father, he'm better now. Joel have put him right. You come over to the pot with me and we'll do up some soup."

That night Joel sat with his father, and well before dawn he set out for Newlyn. Hab and Rose had gone back to their cottage. Mother and Obadiah were still asleep. Father had been restless, but, for the most, he'd slept. He was still in a shallow sleep when Joel left.

Outside the mist had lifted, although there was no moon and the journey across the downs was slow. It was still dark when he reached Redruth.

Already men and bal maidens were heading for the mines. Merchants and itinerant workers had set out for their jobs in and around the town.

The Van was harnessed, parked outside a coaching inn. At the rear they were loading goods and sheep, along with cages of chicken; while a cluster of men and women waited at the front, stamping their feet, buffing their hands against the cold.

It was a new idea to run Vans. It had come with the opening of the turnpike roads. The Vans were long carts for transporting livestock and goods. They'd been built with sides and a roof. There was a small compartment at the front, allowing for passengers, but Joel had been on a Van before. It wasn't something he wanted to endure more often than he had to.

He paid his six pence and clambered into the compartment, although several large ladies and a good few men had climbed in ahead of him. The best part of the space on the two wooden benches were already taken.

One of the women said: "Here, boy, there be room between me and this gentleman." But he had to prise himself in. The woman's hips took up most of the space, while the man made no effort to move. He'd be squashed like this until mid-morning – or later if the Van got into difficulties along the way.

It was almost dark in the compartment. There were slits of windows near the roof, but no glass, and he knew, as soon as the journey started, someone would draw heavy curtains. Then whatever light there was, would be shut out.

After a few minutes the Van began to move. First, a lurch as the horses eased forwards, then a shaking and the rattle of wheels over the cobbled streets. Without a word, a thin, grimly black-coated man with dark beard and tall hat got up and drew the curtains.

Wedged as he was, Joel could hardly breathe; not that breathing was such a good idea. His neighbours didn't give off the smell of Cass's fresh flowers. He was overpowered by a rank, greasy odour, mingled with the stench of sheep and the smell of caged chickens from the compartment behind.

As they trundled over the cobbles, the man beside him began scratching, pushing his hand between himself and Joel to dig into his thigh. After that he started on his stomach, then his legs. His hand went to his head, his neck, his arms. It wasn't long before Joel had the uncontrollable urge to join him.

It seemed an age, too, before they were out in the country, but, when they were, the Van lurched from one side to the other, with the woman being thrown against him as it swung to the right, and the man with his lice and fleas, as it swayed to the left.

All the time the stench of unwashed beings, human and animal, grew, while the temperature in the darkened compartment fell towards freezing. They stopped to drop off goods and pick up more in Camborne and Hayle, then at a few coaching inns and turnpikes. The stops did give passengers the chance to get out and stretch, but, whenever they climbed back, they took the same seats, leaving him squashed between the large lady and the scratching man.

By the time they reached Penzance it was well into morning. The sky was grey, the sea in Mount's Bay, leaden and restless. The whole bay was in constant motion, with waves tapering to foaming crests. He pulled his coat around him against a whipped-up wind that tugged at his hair as he hurried along the coastal path.

If he could get to Newlyn quickly – if he could persuade the Pellar to come back with him on the night Van – they would be with his father and the other men by morning. But he was anxious now. He didn't know much about Rachel Pengelly. He'd heard she was moody and volatile. If she liked him and was feeling sweet, she might come. If she wasn't, it would take a lot of persuading to get her to Redruth.

The path was easy. It couldn't have been more than two miles, but he'd never been this far, and when he got to Newlyn, his intentions were shaken. The harbour was bustling, crowded with fishing boats along with all the activities of a thriving port. There was a quay and salting houses. Fishing gear was piled along the jetty, with cottages packed tightly around the harbour. Yet more clung to the hill. Men and boys were working on nets and crab pots. The occasional cart trundled over the cobbled road. It was so much bigger than he'd expected, and he had no idea where the Pellar lived.

Near where he stood was a fisherman crafting a crab pot. Joel moved towards him.

"You looking for someone?" the man said.

"I got to find the Pellar, Rachel Pengelly," said Joel. "I do need her for my father."

"Where you from, boy?" the man asked.

"Redruth. Wheal Gwenvor. We had an accident over there a couple of days back – in the mine. A lot of men was hurt."

"She'm getting on a bit now, the Pellar," said the fisherman, shaking his head. "She ain't in the flush of youth no more. It ain't likely she'll go as far as Redruth."

It had never occurred to him that she might be too old to make the journey. "I got to try," he said. "We got big trouble back home. It's only the Pellar what can do anything about it."

He watched the man rest a hand on his pot and look across to the hill. "You best go and see her then. She do live up there. The last cottage at the top. You won't have no trouble finding it."

On the hill there were cottages and houses set each side of the road, crammed in on each other, with a cobbled path between them. A ditch ran down the centre of the path, shining wet with waste and effluence.

When he reached the summit, he found a small, whitewashed cottage, with a window on either side of a central door. The bottom half of the door was closed, although the top swung open. There were two cats curled on the doorstep, both black. As Joel got near they half opened their eyes – cold, greenish-yellow eyes, bilious and malicious. Without moving they stared at him.

He took a deep breath, knocking on the half open door. His heart thumped as he heard a rustle of movement from inside. A stooped old woman appeared. Her skimpy grey hair hung, bedraggled, to her shoulders. Her leathery face was brown, wrinkled to the texture of a walnut shell. Her eyes narrowed as she stared at him. They were piercing blue, gleaming out between puffed eye sockets. Her mouth sank into her cheeks and she chewed relentlessly on her gums. The black, loosely crocheted shawl she wore was streaked with bits of grey hair.

"And whose young man are you?" she demanded.

"My father be Amos Penberthy, ma'am. But we don't live around here."

"I didn't think you did, boy," she said. "Pretty face like yours – I'd have remembered."

"Are you the Pellar?" he asked.

She looked at him suspiciously. "I been known to lift the evil eye from a few unfortunate people, but it don't come easy, with age crippling me and the rheum in every limb."

"I'm real sorry about the rheum," Joel said. "Because I got sore need of you back home. My father and other men, they'm dying, and it were all my fault." He didn't know how to deal with this old woman, but he clung to the hope that, because she said he was pretty, he might soften her. He told her about the curse and reading from the book, while she just stood there, chewing her gums. When he'd finished, she said, "That weren't a very clever thing to do, were it? And where be all these poor souls what you told me about?"

"They do live a long way from here, ma'am," Joel said. "But we believe it's only you what can help. It be over Wheal Gwenvor, down by Redruth."

She still didn't move, and her cold blue eyes hardly flinched. "That's a mighty way for an old woman to go, with the rheum and the age what's crept up on her. But I suppose you got a coach and six handsome white horses down by the harbour so you can take me in style. Is that right, boy?"

He smiled shyly, and she smiled back, a grin that showed the brown stumps embedded like tombstones in her ageing gums.

"No ma'am, it ain't no carriage and horses. It's only the Van from Penzance, but my brother Hab, and his wife, they said you could stay at their cottage while you'm with us."

Her face shrank into a scowl. "I'd rather be put up in the coaching inn, boy. I know what miners' cottages are like. At my age I need all the comforts of good living."

"That be all right, Miss Pengelly," he said. "I got money put by. You can have the coaching inn if that be what you want, only – please say you'll come."

Suddenly she said: "You'm a sweet boy. I wouldn't be doing this if you wasn't, not at my time of life, but, as it be you what's asking, I'll do it. I need my things though, my pot and my potions, and it'll be you what do carry them. It'll take a long time getting across to Penzance, too." She turned towards the darkened room. "You wait here, while I get what I do need."

Then she disappeared.

When she came to the door again, she was carrying a twisted cane of ash. She handed him a heavy cast-iron pot, filled with small bags. After that she grasped his arm. "You'll have to take my weight, boy," she said. "You and the stick. And you got to show patience. But we'll get there, because a man what can father a pretty boy like you, he do deserve the Pellar's help."

Chapter 8

She leaned heavily on Joel's shoulder across the bay. Her pot weighed him down, although she took a lot of breaks, giving him time to rest. It was very close to evening when they reached Penzance.

She didn't say a lot, but he could sense her mood was changing. The strain on her ancient limbs was making her irritable. By the time they reached the Van she was snapping every time she spoke.

He managed to wedge her between two women, although, when the coachman wanted to stow her pot in the back, it set her off on a string of abuse. "You'm a cretin, mister," she growled. "That pot do stay with me. Put it between my feet, and if you try to shift it out the back, I'll strike you with the plague."

The Pellar insisted on straddling the pot with her legs, and that skewed both women towards the corners of the coach.

There wasn't any room for him. He had to sit with the coachman at the front, but he didn't mind. It meant he escaped being stuck in that tiny compartment with the fug of foul smells.

The Van lurched with every rut and pothole, while the wind blew into squally showers. By the time they reached Redruth he was frozen, but the Pellar's mood had become even darker.

She was grumbling about the God-forsaken place she'd been dragged to, claiming her body was too stiff to move. He helped her from the Van, carrying her pot and potions into the inn – where the landlord demanded a night's payment in advance.

He'd brought coins from his savings, although the cost took every penny. The man wanted more, too, to be paid the next day, covering the whole week. Joel knew he could manage. He'd always carried a hope that, one day, he'd find someone like Rose. He knew, to set up home he'd need money. In the good times he'd put by all he could spare.

He left the Pellar installed by a blazing fire, with a bowl of soup. But, when he got home, his father was tossing, calling out in a delirium again. Obadiah ran to him sobbing, "Make him better like you done last night, Joel."

He looked at his father's sweat-drenched face and cracked lips. "How long have he been like this?" he said.

"We done all we could," said his mother. "Rose and Hab only come over late this evening. I been dousing his face with water, and we couldn't let the fire go down – he do need the warmth."

No matter how tired he was, getting his father right was the only thing that mattered.

He forced his hands to undress him, wiping his body with damp cloths, while Rose fed him water.

But there was an even greater stench from the leg. The flesh around the wound was livid, while the gash was weeping. He'd got to the Pellar just in time. If the healing didn't begin soon, he knew Father would die. He washed and bound the wound. Then he said, "Try and feed him some soup, Mother. Just a drop to keep his strength up."

Rose ladled two bowls. "I'll feed him," she said. "And I put some out for you, boy. You'll be starving."

"He sat up all night with Father," said his mother. "Then – going down Newlyn – and – doing all this to get Father right when he got back – the boy's a saint."

Rose began spooning the soup into his father's mouth. "I'll sit with him tonight," she said. "You get some sleep in."

Hab hadn't spoken. He'd torn rags to bind the wound, but he'd been silent, glowering at Joel.

"Did the Pellar come?" he said at last.

"She'm in the coaching inn, down Redruth," said Joel. "Tomorrow, early, I got to fetch her over here."

"Well, let's hope, for your sake, she can do something," his brother snarled. He stood up, turning towards the door. "I'm off out. I suppose I best come back here when I'm done, seeing as Rose be sitting with Father. But you know this, Joel Penberthy. Feelings is running high down that mine. If the Pellar don't do nothing about this curse, then life is going to be rough on you, that's for certain."

"Where you going?" demanded Rose. "Is it down that ale house again? With your father sick, I would have thought you were better staying here, by him".

"Be quiet, woman, and keep your place," he snapped. "You want to try sweating through a day down that pit with nothing but talk of death and men's lives ruined. You'd be in want for the beer and brandy – and you don't need me here. You got the saint to look after Father. I'm out, and I'll be back when I'm done."

"Don't take no notice of him, Joel, boy," his mother said when he'd gone. She brought another damp cloth for Father's face. "You done wonders here today – you got nothing to reproach yourself with. Drink up that soup and get in a good night's sleep. The Pellar will be here in the morning. She'll put Father right."

But, as he lay at the back of the room with Obadiah, he couldn't ignore what Hab had said. All night he was tormented with restless dreams, and the world was hardly stirring when he woke.

Rose was still sitting with Father. She'd been keeping him cool by rinsing his face and arms. Hab had come back late. He was sleeping the brandy off by the fire.

Later Rose and his mother were going to church. It was Sunday. They wanted him to go with them. They said he had to show the world he wasn't a blasphemer, and he could understand how they felt. Like everyone he knew, he'd been brought up to fear God. Church was part of life – the same as eating or sleeping. But today he was more anxious to get the Pellar to Father.

A breeze cut in from the west as he set out, with the clouds, low and squally.

He found Rachel Pengelly sitting with her shawl draped over her shoulders. She was chewing at a crust of bread and sipping a dish of tea. There was no Van on Sundays – as it was God's holy day. The town was quiet… but that couldn't be said of the Pellar. She was in a rip of a mood, complaining that the bed was lumpy, that she'd hardly slept, that the soup she'd been given last night was just water and turnips, and the bread she was eating was stale and mouldy.

"Ain't there another Inn I could move to, boy?" she demanded. "This place ain't fit for dogs."

"You could stay with Hab and Rose," he reminded her.

"A miner's hovel. That ain't no place for the Pellar," she snorted. She staggered out of her chair, grabbing her pot. "I suppose I'd better come back here." Then she turned to the landlord. "But I want a fresh bed, mister, with a decent mattress. I will not sleep another night on that bag of rocks."

Joel was half afraid the landlord would refuse to have her back. "It's all right, Miss Pengelly," he said. "You let me take your pot, like yesterday. You can lean on my arm. Rose will have a good bowl of soup for you when we get to Father's."

"It be still night out there, boy," she growled. "How am I meant to see my way in that blackness?"

"I know the way," he said. "You just lean on me."

As they struggled over the downs, she complained about the hills and hedges and the squally weather. The mood she'd shown when they were back in Newlyn seemed to have melted like summer snow. By the time they reached the cottage she was very dark tempered, and what was worse, she was remembering more frequently that it was him who'd brought the curse down on all the men.

Rose, Obadiah and his mother had already left for church. Hab had been put with Father – and with Rose gone, there would be no soup.

When she reached the cottage door, the Pellar stood, sniffing. "There be a smell about this place, boy," she said. She was scowling and her words made Joel uneasy. "I'm thinking it's bigger than any potion what the Pellar's carrying. I doubt there be runes enough to cure an evil as foul as what's here. And it was you what brought it about too, by my reckoning."

As soon as she'd said it, Hab called from the cottage, "You'm right, ma'am. It's the boy's fault. I told him, he brought a curse down on our people what ain't going to be lifted."

When she made Hab out, her mood seemed to change. "Who might you be?" she said.

"Hab, ma'am – Habakkuk Penberthy. That runt be my brother."

Straight away she hobbled over, gripping him by the arm, and the grin Joel had seen in Newlyn was back on her wrinkled old face. "The boy, here, I don't believe he mentioned you." She looked him up and down. "You cut a fine figure," she added. "Very handsome. There be more muscle on you than what the boy got. You, with your head of lovely black hair and your fine stature. Is it your father what be lying there?" She peered down. "Bring a candle, boy, so I can see what I'm about."

All Joel could do was sink into a corner. He watched, while Hab fetched the candle.

"Now, water for my pot, and put it on the fire, boy. You can heat it, ready for my potions."

It was Hab who fed the fire, placing the pot on the trivet.

Joel watched as she shook her head. "Your father, he'm in a bad way," she said. "I don't like the look nor the smell of him. I got to say, boy, death be in the air – a curse what weigh down so heavy the Pellar can't see she can shift it."

"That don't surprise me, ma'am," he said. His voice hinted triumph. "The runt, here, he'm a bad lot. It was him what caused the accident down the mine on top of bringing the curse on. He'm a dreamer. You take one look at him. He ain't a proper man. He got the look of a maid about him. That ain't how God do make men. He ain't right in the head, neither. I always knew that, but Mother and Father, they don't see it."

The Pellar turned towards Joel. Now her eyes were sharp. "He'm a pretty boy," she said. "But I'm thinking, may be you'm right. If he'm the devil's child, the devil do make his children pretty – That way they fool the likes of you and me."

There was nothing Joel could do or say. But worse, it looked as if the old woman wasn't going to make his father better. She didn't touch the wounded leg. All she did was brush his father's face. When her pot had boiled she put in herbs and potions. Then she muttered a kind of chant. She ladled some of her brew into a bowl, pouring the rest into a jug, and she told Hab, "Feed him a drop every morning and every night." She also put both hands on Father, muttering more words – but they didn't make any sense – and Joel suspected they wouldn't make any difference. At last she turned and said, "I done what I can here, boy, but I don't hold out no hope. That runt's curse be potent – Now I want for you to lead me to them other sick folk. It's you what must carry the pot. It be too heavy for my old arms. And you must be my companion. It be down to you to help me rid this place of the evil what that young whelp have brought on these poor people."

Hab moved towards the door, leading the old woman into the morning's greyness, while Joel stared after them. Finally he crept across to kneel by the pallet, gripping his father's hand. "Don't you take no notice of that old crone, Father," he whispered. "There ain't no smell of death around here, because you ain't going to die. I won't let you, and that's a promise."

His father didn't move. But his eyes half opened… and just for a moment there was the flicker of a smile.

When he got to the pit next morning he could sense a darker feeling. Bal maidens turned their heads. Men ignored him. Others spat. He heard one mutter: "I'm off. There be company around here and I don't fancy having it nowhere near me."

At last he caught sight of Rose crossing the yard. As soon as she saw him she came over. "Joel, boy," she said.

"I wouldn't stay around if I was you. That witch and your brother been laying the poison. George Laity died last night. The Pellar be putting it about that you'm to blame." It was all fitting with what he'd heard the previous day, and there was so little he could do to resist it. He knew, though, running away wasn't the answer.

"I got to stay, Rose," he said. "With Father sick we do need the money. I got to work with these people."

"It's a pity you ever brought that woman back here," she said. "I don't see she'm doing no good. She don't help your cause, neither. She'm a fickle piece of wickedness."

"I got to work, though," he persisted.

"Trouble is, Joel, men are saying they ain't working with you." She looked across at the groups gathered at the pithead. "It's going to be real hard for you down there."

"Ain't there nobody what's getting better?" he asked.

She shook her head. "Nothing's been said."

"I got to stay," he persisted.

"Well, you be careful. What do rile me is that Sam Eustice, what started all this buffoonery, he'm getting away without a blemish. That ain't right. And as for Hab, I don't know what have got into him. He'm in that Pellar's pocket. She didn't go back to Redruth last night. Her Ladyship decided she'd stay with us after all. Hab said we had to give up our bed for her. We had to sleep on the floor, and she do demand the best of everything. I don't know how I'm going to feed her."

"I got money put by," he said. "You can have that."

He walked anxiously towards the line of men, but they shuffled away. Then, as they began to move towards the shaft, the underground captain caught his eye.

"Tempers be running hot, boy," he said. "And I know it be hard on you, with your father sick."

"He'm holding on, Cap'm Bolitho," he said.

"But it ain't right, what they men are doing. Anyone can see that business down the ale house was Sam Eustice's fault – and the liquor. It would be better if they kept clear of that. But no-one should be blaming you." He looked across at the column of men. "Would you be happier not going down there today?"

"I need the money, Cap'm, with Father bad, and the boy, Obadiah, to keep, and Mother."

"Well, I'm around to see no harm do come to you. If I put you on kibbles and trucks it'll keep you away from they others. If we do that for a few days till the dust settle – then there's Billy Jewell, he'm a good man. You can work with him, but, for the next day or two, you work on your own."

The morning was hard though. Even on kibbles and trucks he was rubbing shoulders with other workers. At croust time he was glad to get away. He felt numbed, and there was the image of his injured father hovering at the back of his thoughts.

He knew that somewhere out there he might find a stope that could take him away from all this. If Cass had seen his note she may be waiting for him. Then there was Ewan, and his invitation back to the cloth village. But it wasn't easy to think about that with the burden of hostility and hate bearing down on him. He resented throwing his crust to the knockers. The Bucca hadn't done anything for him.

At last, though, he began to grope his way back along the level.

But, as he walked, he was climbing again. There were rock falls and rubble, while, ahead of him the light had turned to a steady, white glow.

Chapter 9

The sky was even brighter today. It spread in a deep, unbroken blue; but Cass wasn't there. Joel sat on the tuft of grass, letting the sun's rays soak into him. Then he caught a flash of light from the fissure. He could see the bottle tucked between the stones. The note and the pen had gone. There was a new piece of paper, though. Excitedly he scanned the message. *"Hi, Joel,"* he read. *"What an awesome thrill. You got my note and answered it! I have been up here for the last couple of days, hoping to see you. I will come again every day at one o'clock. If I am not here, could you wait around? I WILL COME, and I've got everything crossed. Please, please be here.*

"Love, Your twenty-first century friend,

Cass X."

He knew about time. The pastor had a clock, and there was one on the church tower, but, here there was no way he could tell what hour it was. In his own world it was croust time – somewhere near mid-day. The shadows here suggested a similar time. Mid-day, he knew, was twelve of the clock. The words Cass had used were 'one o'clock'. He guessed that was their way of saying one of the clock. If he sat here for one hour, she would come.

Being away from the pit wasn't a worry. Working on kibbles, no-one would notice. The underground captain was watching out for him, but the mine was dark. He didn't think even the captain would see he wasn't there. He watched the movements along the roads until there was a rustle among the gorse bushes and Cass emerged. She was wearing a bright red smock, tighter than the one she wore last week, with shorter sleeves. Its fabric was more like the smock Ewan wore.

Her face lit when she saw him, but, beside her there was another person, most certainly a boy – someone her own age, dark haired, slim and clean faced. To Joel, his close cropped hair imitated the spines of a hedgehog. He was wearing a black smock and full-length black britches. Suddenly, seeing him made Joel anxious.

Cass broke into a run. As he stood up, she grabbed him, pulling him towards her, hugging him. "You're here," she said. "That is so amazing. I was dead excited last Friday when I got your note. I've been up every day."

This way, with the hugs, was something he wasn't used to. Without being able to control himself, he pulled back. It made her smile. "Sorry," she said. "I got a bit carried away, didn't I? – That's excitement at seeing you." She half turned towards the boy. "This is my mate, Karl Greaves. His dad's the local GP."

Joel nodded towards him, but the boy's expression still made him uneasy.

"Yeah, good to meet you, mate," the boy said. "Cass has been rattling on about you all weekend. She's got this cracked idea you've come from the eighteenth century."

"I know it ain't natural, coming here," he said. "I been here three times now."

"You reckon?" said Karl. He sat on the tuft of grass. "It's more than unnatural, mate. It's impossible."

Joel could see Cass wasn't pleased. She aimed a kick at the boy. "I've been trying to convince him all weekend, Joel. Tell him about this morning – from when you got up." She sat by Karl, leaving a space between them, patting the outcrop so he would sit down. There was the fragrance of flowers about her again. Even the boy seemed to give off a smell of perfume. It wasn't the same as Cass's, but it was pleasant, a cleansing smell – almost the smell of tree sap. Sitting between them he couldn't help thinking of the Van with the ample lady and the flea-bitten man.

In spite of the boy, something made him want to tell Cass what was happening. It wasn't like last week. Now he was talking to someone who believed what he was saying. "I tended Father," he said. "He was hurt in the accident. I walked to the mine after I done that."

"The accident?" she exclaimed. "You said about that on Thursday, yeah?" She looked at him. "Did it happen then?"

He nodded. "An explosion what brought down the third level. There be anger with the men back there now. The accident was my fault. The underground cap'm, he've put me on kibbles and trucks."

Karl was staring. His eyes were even darker than Cass's, but they still seemed to radiate hostility. "What's a kibble?" he demanded.

"It be like a pail. We do carry the broken gangue in it."

"Yeah?" said Karl. "You could have picked that up on Wikipedia. It doesn't convince me, mate."

By now Cass was getting even more annoyed. "Quit being so aggressive, Karl. Give the guy space." She turned, gripping Joel's hand. "Don't take any notice of him. He's like that about everything."

"Well, it's a con, Cass," Karl said. "The guy will be one of your dad's actors. But, what's freaking me out is, why he'd spin all this crap at all?"

"It isn't crap," Cass insisted. "I mean, when he went into the stope, Thursday, I searched for him. I didn't believe him until then, but he wasn't there. He'd just disappeared."

Joel, though, felt more uneasy with every word. It was as if he was putting a wedge between two friends.

"You'm right," he said suddenly. "It don't make no sense – none of it do. It ain't right, me being here. I just got to go back to my own time, that's all." He stood up, but Cass grabbed his arm.

"No, Joel. Don't you dare. Karl you're a pig. See what you've done?"

"I don't mean to dis you, mate," Karl said, "But – it doesn't happen. It's got to be a sort of dream-world you're in."

"Them words don't mean nothing to me," said Joel. "But you'm right to believe it don't happen. It look like, if I don't go back now, I'll get hate thrown at me wherever I do go."

"You won't, Joel, honest," Cass said, still hanging on to his arm. "I mean, I don't hate you, do I?"

Eventually he sat back on the grass bank, although he still wasn't convinced. There was Ewan. He hadn't shown any hate. "I come here last Friday," he said at last. "I went down Tehidy when I didn't see you. There were a village down there, all cloth dwellings and houses on wheels. I met a boy what was very kind to me. He talked like I was a new friend. He said to go into the village with him. But I didn't do it, not then." He blushed, looking at the slim girl with her brown eyes. "I comed back here. I wanted for you to come."

"Well, there you are then," Cass said. "That'll be Tehidy Holiday Park. Will the boy be there now?"

He nodded. "He said, if I do come by another time, to go and see him. But he don't know I come through no stope. If he know that, he'll say I'm a liar. He'll be hating me like this boy here."

To his amazement, Karl suddenly put a hand on his. "I don't hate you, mate," he said. "And I'm Karl, not 'this boy'. It's just, what you're telling us is like – it's off the scale. I still don't believe it – but, if there's a reason you've dreamed it up..." He looked at Cass. "If the guy's still there, say we go down there. What do you think?"

Cass looked doubtful. "Like Joel said, he doesn't know about him coming through a time warp. If he turns on him like you did..." She looked towards Joel. "What's this guy's name?"

By now going to see Ewan didn't seem such a good idea. But he liked the person he'd met in the cloth village, and if they did go, he'd have Cass with him.

"He'm called Ewan," he said. "He told me he'd be there – staying at something like T eight."

"That'll be his pitch," said Karl.

There wasn't any more discussion. Cass was already leading them down the hill. In no time he could see the cloth village, laid out just as he'd seen it last week. They followed a road to the hill's top, with people lying out in their chairs and on the beds. Some nodded and gave friendly greetings or smiles. But he was nervous. He didn't know how Ewan would react when he told him where he'd come from.

Cass was explaining about camp sites – tents and caravans – about holidays that people enjoyed every year. She said people were paid by their bosses, even when they took the days without working. The strange-shaped carriages, she told him, were cars. You could get from Cornwall to London in six hours if you went in one. In a Van it would take that long to get to Bodmin.

There were camper vans, too, and… The more Joel heard, the more strange and amazing this world seemed, but now, in spite of his fear at seeing Ewan, he was excited by what he saw.

Karl pointed out small wooden flags indicating the pitch numbers. But at 'T eight', they found one of the cottages on wheels – a caravan, with a cloth thing forming a porch. Cass said that was an awning.

Ewan was beyond the awning, lying on a bed similar to the one he'd seen in the cottage garden. He was reading. He looked up as they got near, smiling at Joel, but then he looked puzzled. He scrambled to his feet. "Great to see you, Joel. And... are these your mates?"

Cass's face coloured. "Yeah. It looks like we're gate-crashing a bit, doesn't it? But, OK, we're Joel's friends. We'll explain."

Karl nodded awkwardly, but Ewan just smiled.

"No sweat. My lot have gone to St Michael's Mount and Mousehole for the day. I fancied staying back. I want to go down to Portreath later – get some surfing in. Grab a seat." He pulled three fabric chairs across from the awning, setting them around the bed. "What about a coke? Then we could all go down to Portreath."

Cass led Joel to a chair. "A coke would be great," she said. "But Joel won't have drunk anything like coke before, and he won't have a clue about surfing."

"He knows about surfing," said Ewan. "We talked about it last Friday. That's why you've come back, yeah?"

"You might have said to him about surfing," Cass said, laughing. It seemed she wasn't going to bother about preliminaries before revealing Joel's origins. "He wouldn't have had the least idea what you were on about, though."

Somehow Ewan seemed to be knocked off balance. He looked from Cass to Joel and back, smiling awkwardly, shaking his head. "You've lost me," he said.

Joel was feeling worse with every passing minute, although it looked as though Cass was enjoying it.

"Tell Ewan your story, Joel," she said.

Now though, all he wanted was to go back to the stope. "I can't do that," he said. "It be best if he don't know."

"He's scared you won't believe him," said Cass. But Ewan just looked more puzzled.

"I don't get any of this. Say I get the cokes, then tell me." He turned to Karl. "Can you give us a hand?"

When the boys came back, they were carrying bottles containing a dark ale-coloured liquid. There was a faint haze drifting from the bottles, like steam, but, when Joel took hold of his, it was icy cold. He couldn't begin to grasp how something could be so cold on a day when the weather was so warm.

Karl and Ewan sat down, while Cass took a sip from her bottle. Joel didn't want to try his. He just sat, watching.

"It's like," Cass said. – "well – take a look at what Joel's wearing, Ewan."

Ewan shrugged. "Yeah? Some sort of arty-crafty stuff, like the guy's into pottery or something?"

"No way," laughed Cass. "That's a smock. They wore them in the tin mines. It's stuff they wore over two hundred years ago."

"So?" Ewan said.

It made Joel shrink back, more uneasy by the minute.

"Thing is, Ewan, Joel isn't from our time. It's like, he's been coming through this portal in the mine up the hill. He's an eighteenth-century guy. I mean, I know it's amazing, but he's a piece of walking history."

He saw Ewan lie back on his lounger, and the stare of disbelief on his face sent a shiver through him. He had the look of someone who was being taken for a fool. "You're joking," he said. "That's impossible."

"I thought that," Cass said, "– but I really believe it now. I mean, tell Ewan all about your family – what work you do. Say about your dad."

Joel held the bottle of coke close. The glass was freezing his hand. He was afraid to drink. All eyes were on him, and it was almost worse than being back in the pit. "I can't," he said. "He'm going to say I'm a liar, like Karl do."

Suddenly Ewan laughed. "I would love it if it was true, though. You've got no idea. It would be epic."

Something about the laugh gave him more confidence. He looked at the bottle again. He thought he'd try the drink, but the cold liquid tasted sharp, like broken glass in his mouth. It made him splutter.

"It's the fizz," Cass laughed. "You've never had anything like that, have you?"

He shook his head. He knew he was blushing. But Ewan was urging for more. "Go on. Tell us about your family."

He was still hesitant, but, finally he began to recount the last few days. When he came to the accident and his father's injury though, he was caught with a sudden pain. "He'm going to die," he said. "I won't be working with him no more."

It was the first time he'd actually put words to the fear of his father's death and the prospect of never working with him again. His voice trembled. There were tears burning the edges of his eyes.

Suddenly Cass leapt out of her chair, nudging him to one side. She clasped her arm around him. "Was the injury that bad, Joel? He will get better. You must believe he'll get better."

But her compassion broke him. Tears slid down his cheeks. "He won't," he said. "I put a curse on him and all they other injured men. The Pellar come up from Newlyn. She said the evil eye is that bad, she can't shift it. All them what was injured is going to die. That's what she said."

"What's a Pellar, for God's sake?" said Karl.

"The white witch, Rachel Pengelly. She do lift curses."

"And how come you put this curse on everybody?" he demanded.

Joel told them about the ale house, and reading from the wrong book, but all Karl said was, "So?"

"Well, that be blasphemy against the Lord. It be what brought the curse down."

To his amazement Karl just brushed that aside. "That's rubbish – Superstitious crap. I mean, curses and white witches. What planet are you on, mate?"

No-one Joel knew would question a curse brought down by the Almighty. "But it do work," he said. "Them curses and portents. I knowed there was going to be the disaster in the mine."

Cass gave his shoulder a squeeze. "He did know," she said. "He said about it last Thursday. But how did you know, Joel?"

He explained about the white hare and the black dog, although that didn't impress Karl either. "It's empty twaddle," he said. Then he added, "But what you said about your father… I mean, that bit could be right. And if the guy really is sick – Say you're telling it like, this accident really happened – I mean, if you were from the eighteenth century, this Pellar woman, she wouldn't be any use, would she?"

Cass squeezed Joel's shoulder again. She looked at Karl. "So, you're beginning to believe him now, are you?" she said.

"I don't know about that, but inventing a story about a dying father. The guy's actually crying about it. And his father – say he is hurt – I know it's dead impossible, but if his dad's hurt bad, and he really is in the eighteenth century, he doesn't stand a chance. We could cure the bloke though, with my dad."

Suddenly Cass leapt up. "That is awesome, Karl. We could do that."

It was hard for Joel to grasp. "But... how you going to do it?" he said.

"His dad's a GP. We told you. He's a doctor. He treats sick people," said Cass.

"We could do that for your father," Ewan said. "Get Karl's dad to give you drugs and stuff. He could, like, tell you how to treat him. What's wrong with him anyway?"

What they were saying – how they looked, suddenly it felt as though he mattered, as though his father mattered. "Would them modern potions bring him back?" he said. He still had tears burning his eyes. "He was hit by rocks. They smashed his leg – split the bone. He got a foul gash full of filth, and he do sweat. He talk mad things with the delirium. If that wound don't heal, he'm going to die."

Cass was beside him again, bringing her arm around him in a hug. "We'll do it," she said.

"It sounds like the wound's gone septic," Karl told him. "Give him antibiotics – we can cure that. What do you reckon, Ewan?"

"I think it's awesome," Ewan said. "Curing some guy who's living two hundred years ago, through a time portal... and Joel here – I want to believe what he's saying. I really do. It's like hearing something out of a fantasy world, OK – and it's mad, but I just want to believe the guy." He laughed, adding: "It would be a big one for my dad to get his head around. That's for sure."

"Why?" said Karl.

"He works at the Home Office. His job is dealing with migrants, but I'll bet he's never had to cope with a migrant from the eighteenth century."

"Well, what are we going to do?" Cass said. "Should we go over to the surgery now – see your dad, Karl?"

Karl looked at Joel.

"Do you wash and dress your father's wound, Joel?" he said. "Do you keep him cool, to lower the fever?"

He nodded. What Karl had just asked excited him. It was as if he understood what Joel was trying to do. "Every day I do that," he said.

"Will he last out another day, do you think?"

"If it be God's will, I think..."

"Well, let's hope it is God's will," said Karl. "You keep the treatment going tonight, mate. I'll talk to my dad – me and Cass. I'll need Cass, because I still can't get my head around it – I mean, I can't go saying we've got this bloke who's turned up from the eighteenth century, but Cass believes it. Would you be able to come back tomorrow? We'll need tonight, though, to get Dad's mind-set sorted. He's a bit 'last century', my dad is."

"If I can find the stope tomorrow. I never know if it be there," Joel said. "But, what you'm doing..."

"It's what my dad does," said Karl. "All doctors do. And the drugs are guaranteed to work."

"I can't hardly believe it. You really got potions what will make Father better?"

"Sure," Karl said.

Joel lifted the coke bottle to his lips, taking a drink. He swallowed without choking, while the others clapped. But he didn't know what to say or do. He'd already been here too long. He had to get back to kibbles and trucks. Here, though, they'd given him his first real hope that his father would live. These friends believed in their medicines... and their world, it was so full of amazing, miraculous things. "I wish my life were here," he said suddenly, "but I got to go back. I got the day to work out, and I got to see Father's all right."

"Shall we go up the hill with him?" said Ewan. "Like – see him off?"

"If you do that," Joel said, "I'd be real glad."

They left the empty coke bottles and the chairs, making their way down towards the woods. "What if this portal Cass said about closes," said Ewan. "What would you do then?"

"I got to pray that don't happen," he said.

"Could anyone go through? Could we try?" asked Cass.

"Nobody never comed through in my time – nobody but me," he said. "But it ain't like it is here. It be hard back there. If they saw people like you, they'd be certain to put you in gaol. They might even kill you."

They didn't speak again until they reached the mouth of the stope. Then Cass took Joel's hand. "We *will* make your father better. You know that, don't you?" she said. After that she kissed him on the cheek, and to his amazement Ewan put his arms around him in a hug – so did Karl.

"It's been unreal," Ewan said. "Would it be OK if I came tomorrow?"

"I never seen people like you before," said Joel. "Truer friends than I ever knowed. If you could all come tomorrow I'd be proper glad."

Cass whispered: "That is so sweet."

But time was racing. He had to go.

Behind him were voices. “Bye, Joel,” and when he turned around, they were there, three dear friends, stumbling into the stope, trying to follow him. But then their images faded and he turned towards the black descent.

Chapter 10

That night, when he came to grass, Rose was waiting, but she was on her own. "Why ain't Hab here?" he said.

She sniffed. "He didn't come to work today. He'm with that witch what he's so besotted with. It's just you and me, boy, so go down the engine pool and get washed. Then we got to get back to Father."

They didn't speak much on the way. Joel was too full of memories and hopes.

When they came to the cottage, the flicker of candlelight gave him that sign; that his father was still alive, but inside, the air was stifling – with fumes of peat, and the stench of foetid flesh. Father was restless on his pallet. He was slipping into garbled nonsense and he was hot and sweating again.

His mother brought water and fresh clothes. Then she stood behind Joel, clasping her hands. "He don't seem to be getting no better, Joel, boy. I been feeding him the Pellar's potions, but there ain't no sign they'm making no difference."

Joel was moving his father onto his side. "Can't we slip that cloth away, what he been lying on?" he said. "Put down fresh straw? He been on that straw since last week."

"There'm straw out the back," his mother said, turning to Obadiah. "Fetch it in, boy."

As they moved him to take the cloth away, his father groaned; but there was a lot boiling in Joel. Suddenly he said: "I know how to put Father right." He couldn't keep it to himself any longer. "That Pellar, her cures ain't doing nothing. But there be cures I can get what's going to work better than anything the Pellar can give. I met these people.

They got potions. I'm bringing them back tomorrow. They'll take the fever out of Father and cure they wounds."

Rose and Obadiah were sliding out the old straw, piling fresh onto the pallet, while his mother had gone over to the fire to unfold a clean cover. He saw her stiffen. "What you saying, boy?" she snapped. "It be known the Pellar is the only white witch what got potions to lift curses. There ain't nothing a boy like you can do what's better than her. If she get wind of that kind of nonsense she won't do nothing for Father. I've heard tell she got a fiery temper."

"The Pellar ain't doing nothing, Mother," Joel said. "You can see that. But a boy I met today got a father who's a great physician. He do know about potions what would cure Father. The boy told me he'll give them me tomorrow."

His mother bustled across with the cloth. "What kind of foolishness is that?" she said. "Who you been seeing? Some boy down the pit? Because that's where you been all day. You'm telling me you got a boy down there who got a father what's a great physician? You tell me how a great physician is having to send his boy down the pit?"

"It wasn't down no pit," said Joel. "I can't say where I seen him, but tomorrow he'll give me potions." He smoothed his father's face, lying his head back on the fresh straw. "You believe me, don't you, Father? You know I ain't going to let you slip away, not like that Pellar would."

His father opened his eyes, and there was a look on his face that made Joel's soul burn. It was a look of trust, and a kind of softness he'd never seen in his father before. Now there was nothing going to stop him getting to Karl tomorrow.

He'd barely laid the cloth, though, when the Pellar and Hab pushed through. The Pellar staggered to a chair, while Hab laid the pot and potions on the floor. "Horace Tierney's dead," he snarled. "That be two more gone now, boy."

The old woman grunted. "There be a limit to what the Pellar can do. Some of they men show sign of shaking off the curse, where it hasn't took so much hold, but one or two, the Tierney man for one, they got the evil eye too bad. Nothing's going to lift the curse off of them."

Joel was trying to put his mind into Karl's head. He thought Karl would have argued that, if some of the men were recovering, it had nothing to do with the Pellar. They'd been dealt slighter injuries. Nature was working to cure them. Horace Tierney had been badly injured. That was why he'd died. He didn't think Karl would have allowed that the deaths had anything to do with a curse, although he was sick to hear what had happened. He knew he was the one who'd brought the accident about. Whichever way he looked at it, that was a guilt he could never shake off, but, if Karl was right, it wouldn't be the evil eye that killed him.

The Pellar crossed to his father and shook her head. "Still the same," she said. Then she turned to Joel. "Nothing I do is going to lift the curse off of him – not after what you done."

"I washed him and changed the straw. I tended the wound," he said. "He ain't going to die."

"And what can you do that will make a difference?" she demanded. "You, what layered the curses on him. Like your brother said, you spawn nothing but evil." She glanced towards Hab. "Bring me that jug with the potion, boy. I'll give him the treatment, but I do know about these things. Of all the men I treated, it be wasted on him. What chance do he have when he fathered the son of the devil? It be ordained. He'll pay the price."

It was the first time his mother had heard the old woman's pronouncements about the devil. She swung around with a look of defiance. "Joel's a good boy," she said. "No boy could have done more to save his father."

But the Pellar just spat on the floor. "You been bewitched, woman. You can't see the evil what's standing in front of you. Your other son, the handsome one with that lovely black hair, he do see it."

She began to give his father the potions, muttering her strange chant, but now Joel didn't want to believe anything she did or said. In a moment of heat he said: "He ain't going to die, because I can get potions what will take that fever away. I can heal the wound. If Father be still alive tomorrow, I'm getting the cure."

In all his life he'd never seen the blackness he saw in the Pellar's face then. She stopped what she was doing, with her hand lifted over his father, her mouth chewing at her gums, the strands of greying hair shadowing her features. Her lips sank into her jaw, and the slits of blue from her eyes were shooting fire. For a moment she didn't speak. Then she said, "You – get potions? Wield magic over your father what's greater than the Pellar's? You, without a Christian bone in your body? Where you getting these potions, boy – things what will set you above the Pellar?"

"I'm getting them," he said. "I do know someone."

That made her spit on the floor again. "What creature be giving you these potions?"

"A friend," he said.

Her eyes narrowed, and she began to form a cross with her arms. "I can see what you done, child. As clear as day I can see it. You'm sold whatever soul you got to your master, the devil. You tell me, boy. Name me potions what be stronger than the Pellar's?"

He had to think desperately. Some name Karl had given him? At last it came to him. "They be antibiotics – that's what my friend said."

The old woman gave a horse laugh. "I know about these things. They be the products of Satan."

Joel's mother was sitting, frozen, with her eyes staring. "Can't you see what that child have done, woman?" the Pellar demanded. "He'll be damned to hell if you don't put a stop to his foolery, and he'll take your husband along with him."

She hobbled over to Hab. Then she swung around with a look of cunning that scared Joel. "The Pellar know how he might cure his father," she said. She rested heavily on her stick. "Maybe he could save his own soul too, but he won't do it. The boy be too steeped in wickedness. The remedy be there though. It's a great penance. Tomorrow, instead of going down that mine, boy, you walk to the church in Illogan – barefoot so the ground do shred your feet. When you'm there, you find the pastor – take the prayer book. Then read a proper prayer for your father, in front of God's own altar. If you do that, maybe the Lord will show mercy on you and free you from the devil's grip. Maybe he'll take the curse away. But that be the only thing you can do to save your father. There ain't no cure you can bring consorting with Satan."

His mother was looking at him and her expression had changed. "Do it boy," she said. "Do what the Pellar do say. That way you can save your father and save your own soul."

It stunned him. How could he do it? There was Karl – what he'd said – and the potions from Karl's father.

He looked at his own father, lying on the pallet, hardly moving, then at the others. They were all staring at him, their faces dim in the tallow flame, his mother begging with her eyes, Rose seeing the thread of hope, Hab and the Pellar challenging him. There was a triumphant look on the Pellar's face.

But, these people – with the carriages that could get from Tehidy to London in less time than it would take him to get to Bodmin – these people, with their knowledge and wisdom, they didn't believe in the Pellar. They said there was no such thing as a curse.

"No," he said suddenly. "I ain't doing that, not tomorrow. Tomorrow I'm getting them potions, because it be them what will make Father better."

"Just what I said," rasped the Pellar. "I knew the boy wouldn't do it. He'm steeped in Satan's wickedness."

His mother looked at him. "Joel, boy, what are you saying? The Pellar, she've given you the Christian way, the way what will make your peace with God, and you'm telling us you'm going off on some fool's errand to… where? Is the Pellar telling the truth, boy? Is it the devil what you'm consorting with, to refuse to do the penance?"

"He don't care about Father," Hab snarled. "It's what I always said. He ain't right in the head."

"Do it, boy," pleaded Rose. "Go on the walk. See the pastor, for the sake of your poor father."

Everything was twisting in him, but there was a passion burning like it had never burned. "It *is* for Father," he said. "If I thought walking barefoot would help Father, I'd walk to London and back, but that ain't going to do nothing. Look at him. If something don't get done soon he'll be dead before the week's out."

The Pellar was standing there, her wrinkled old face set, her skeins of grey hair hanging limp and bedraggled. In fury he pointed at her. "She won't do nothing. She be willing Father to die. These people though, they'm good people. They want for him to live."

"I've always took you for a good boy," his mother said.

"I am a good boy. I love my father. Can't you see that, Mother? Can't you see it, Rose? It is for Father. That be why I'm doing this."

"Your father wouldn't thank you for selling your soul to no devil," his mother said. "See sense, boy."

They were all staring at him, unable to understand what was driving him. Even Rose's stare was pushing at him. "I am seeing sense," he said at last. "They potions. That's what sense is." But then he flinched. There was a look in his mother's eye – and he knew that look. If she was riled she had a temper – and when her tongue was let loose...

"There be only one sense what I can see," she snapped. "You won't do no penance for reading out of that evil book. You won't make no peace with Almighty God. What you'm doing is going off in search of some folk what the Pellar said is in hock with the devil, people with potions what she wouldn't touch." She paused, her face dark with a sudden pain and anger. "That ain't the son I gived birth to – the son what I brought up to fear the Lord. You being like you are, boy, I don't know – you can't be no son of mine, not if you'm saying and doing things like that."

He stared, taking in the triumphant looks of Hab and the Pellar. Rose had turned away, Obadiah whimpered in the corner – and he felt the sting in his mother's words. "If that be what you think of me, Mother," he said, "then I ain't staying under this roof. But you'm wrong, all of you. I love my father. I ain't going to see him die. Tomorrow I'll be back, and I'll have them cures."

He was already making for the door, but his mother called after him. She was like that. Her tongue would get the better of her, then, straight away, she would relent. "Joel, boy, stay. I was hasty. Don't go into them fields tonight."

Her words had cut him through to his soul, though. "I'm going," he said. "But I'll be back tomorrow, and tomorrow I'll put Father right."

He grabbed his croust bag, pushing into the biting air, shutting the door; and he wouldn't go back. He wouldn't cross into that cottage again until he could prove that the potions worked – and that he hadn't sold his soul to the devil.

Chapter 11

For a while he paced across the downs, but now he was out in the night's chill he was having doubts. He'd been brought up to think the way Hab and his mother thought, the way Rose and the pastor thought; that God controlled everything. He'd been brought up to believe God would punish the wrongdoer and the foolish. God gave and God took away. He'd been told that, when God took away, that was the curse. But now he'd met Karl, and Karl said all that was nonsense. Because Karl's and Cass's world was so amazingly different, he'd thrown his hopes in with them. What made him do that? He'd stood against the Pellar and his mother and Rose. What if he was standing against God?

He walked on until the salt of the sea moistened his face and he heard the waves crashing. For some time he stood at the cliff edge, looking towards the void of the ocean, letting the pain ease until the doubts subsided and he had nothing left except a determination to fight them – Hab, the Pellar, his mother, Rose… What his three friends had said held so much more hope for Father. In the morning he would go to the mine. He would find the stope. He would get to this new time, to his friends, and these potions.

He arranged his croust bag to make a pillow. Then he sorted ferns and scrub, pulling his coat around him. As he curled into a ball against the cold, the only image from the cottage that stayed with him was the look on his father's face when he'd told him he wouldn't let him die. But the chill gnawed his body, along with the damp and the spray from the broken waves. He couldn't sleep. It was only instinct that told him when it was morning and time to go to the mine.

The night had made him stiff, with the moisture soaking through his clothes so that his britches chafed. At the pithead he was tempted to take a wash in the engine pool – but he didn't want to draw attention to himself so, quickly, he changed into his miners' smock, leaving his shirt and britches under cover, hoping they would dry through the day.

There was still barely a crack of light in the sky; only the stains of sulphurous fire from the engine house. Shadows of men and women moved around him. Then he saw Rose. She was alone again and searching him out. At first he thought it might be bad news about Father. But she had a pasty, wrapped in cloth. She pushed it into his croust bag. "Here, boy," she said. "Your mother sent it. She been sick with worry all night. She know she was hasty when she said what she did. It was that Pellar woman goading her. She didn't mean none of it… only..." she sighed, looking at the line of workers. "Why can't you do it, Joel? We know you haven't sold your soul to no devil, but, your mother and me, we can't see it. Why won't you do the penance for the sake of your father, if not for your own sake? We thought you loved your father."

"I do love him, Rose," he said.

The men in the queue were pushing past. Some ignored him, while others shoved him as they went. One muttered, "You want to be a bit more picky what company you do keep, Rose Penberthy."

He closed his eyes. He was too weary to be bothered with that. "Can't you see," he said. "If I go on the Pellar's penance, I won't be doing Father no good. I won't be getting they medicines. I gived my word I'd come back for them today. Good people are waiting for me, and – they potions – these people said they'll cure Father."

"But, Joel," Rose said. "Who are these folk – if you ain't consorting with the devil?"

He shook his head. "I can't tell you. You wouldn't believe me, not even if I did." He looked around, lowering his voice. "But that Pellar, she ain't doing nothing, not for none of them. She couldn't save Horace Tierney nor George Laity. She laid the blame on me because she didn't want to take no blame herself. Them what be getting better, I believe they'd have got better even if she hadn't been putting her potions about. You can't trust her, Rose."

Rose sniffed. "She's a scheming piece of goods and that's for certain. She got Hab wrapped around her little finger – and half the people here, come to that. She'm dangerous, boy." But she still looked anxious. "I wish you'd tell us who it is, though, what you'm consorting with. It don't make no sense to keep it secret."

He turned for the mine. "I can't," he said. "You got to trust me, Rose, and I'll see you tonight."

No-one spoke as he went back to the queue. Today more boys had been put on kibbles and trucks. Some of the tut workers had started opening a new level. It meant there was more rubble and slag to be shifted.

Walter Bolitho was sending boys to their tasks. When he saw Joel he said, "How's Father?" He glanced around, lowering his voice. "And you, boy. Are you doing all right?"

"Thank you, Cap'm. Father be much the same – and working on trucks and kibbles I can keep clear of they men most of the time."

"Good boy," the captain said. "You carry on in the second level. I'll send most of they scoundrels down further, out your way."

Down at the rock face boys were crouched, fanning at candles, trying to coax a flame. The sound of hammers on jumping bars rang in his ears, along with the rhythm of picks, and the steady rumble of trucks. At croust time he nibbled his pasty, watching the limp flame up by the others. He heard the murmur of their voices. Then, throwing his crust for the knockers, he whispered, "Bucca, find me the stope. I got to save my father."

Then he groped his way along the level, feeling for the walls, until the floor began to rise.

He came out just as his three friends appeared from a cluster of trees.

This time Joel didn't wait. He ran towards them. Cass and Karl were leaning on strange devices – structures on two wheels, and the way they leaned suggested they needed them for support. Ewan was walking without a device.

Cass threw her device to the ground when she saw him, and held him in a hug. "I was so afraid, last night, you wouldn't make it," she said. "And your father? Is he OK?"

Today he didn't move away. "I think he've been spared through the night," he told her.

The two boys gave him the big, expansive hugs of their time, but Ewan looked at him. "Are you all right?" he said. "You look a bit rough."

"I didn't get no sleep. I was out on the cliffs all night," he explained.

"Why?" Cass asked, picking up her support device.

"I said to my family about they cures what you was giving me. It stirred up trouble. I wouldn't stay in the house."

He told them about the Pellar and the penance, but it looked as if steam was building inside Karl. "That is such a load of crap," he said.

"I wouldn't give in," said Joel. "Then, my mother, she turned on me."

Cass glanced at the others. "Shouldn't we go back to my place? Let him shower and clean up?"

He didn't know what that was, but Karl didn't want it to happen. "We've fixed to see dad at one," he said. "And..." He glanced at Joel. "I've got to tell you this, Joel, mate. Dad's agreed to see you, but we couldn't convince him you'd come through a time portal." He turned to Cass again. "It would be better if he didn't look too smart. The rougher he is, the more likely we are to get through to Dad."

"Might he not give me them potions?" Joel demanded, anxiously.

But Karl just grinned. "We'll make sure he does. I mean, he's a good guy really, my dad. Don't kid yourself it'll be easy, though. He reckons you're delusional. He wasn't that pleased we'd got involved with you, to be honest."

This wasn't the assurance Joel needed. Without the potions his father would die, but he didn't voice his fears, and Karl did seem confident they'd persuade the great physician.

As they reached Polgwenvor, setting out along the raised pathway, he kept well towards the hedge. Even with the others there, the speed of the things on the road terrified him. If one wandered onto the path he was certain they'd all be killed. His three friends worked hard to lift his spirits, and soon his attention was back on Karl and Cass with those devices. "Is you hurt in some way?" he asked.

Cass frowned. "Why?"

"Well, them things what you'm resting on, to help you walk..."

Suddenly she burst out laughing. So did Karl and Ewan.

"Our bikes, you mean?"

"Is that what they'm called?"

"We ride them," said Karl. "It's a bit of a drag from Cass's house, especially as we had to go to Tehidy to pick up Ewan."

Joel was still clouded with tiredness. He wasn't sure he'd understood. "You said you do ride them things?" he exclaimed. "But they ain't going to stand up, not if you wasn't holding on to them. You'd fall over, for certain."

"It's just a matter of balance," said Ewan. "Show him, guys."

All at once Cass and Karl pushed their devices onto the road, mounting them as if they were mounting horses. Within seconds they were speeding away, and there wasn't so much as a wobble.

Joel breathed in. "That be like the acrobats down Redruth fair," he gasped.

Ewan was laughing even more now. "Nearly every kid in the country can ride a bike," he said. "See how much faster it is than walking."

It was another amazing thing in this strange new world, but this time it was one that Joel didn't want any part of. There was no way he could mount one of those without taking on some serious injury.

He watched as Karl and Cass turned to ride back. "Joel thinks you're acrobats," Ewan said. "He thinks you'd be a big hit at Redruth fair."

Cass flashed him a smile. "Glad you're impressed."

Then they began to walk along the raised pathway again, just pushing their bikes. A few people nodded to Karl, but no-one seemed to notice Joel. His friends were showing him points of interest; shops and schools and other buildings. What they told him seemed hard to believe, especially when they explained schools. Every child in the country was taught to read and write, and that amazed him. There were no schools for people like him. He'd been lucky that the pastor had singled him out.

They ambled on until they came to what they called 'a crossing' – a series of thick, white dashes across the road. They explained that all the cars and lorries would stop for them. But he wouldn't move until there was a lull in the traffic. Then he grabbed Cass by the hand and ran, dragging her with him, while his heart raced.

Where they'd crossed, a large, square house stood in its own grounds. Beside it was an area covered with the same surface as the road. There were grassy bits, with patches of earth where shrubs and flowers grew; but a bigger piece of road surface lay to their right with a row of cars standing on it.

Beyond the cars was a white, flat-roofed building with large, clear glass windows. "That's my dad's surgery," Karl told him. "That's where we're going."

Seeing the building rekindled the fear. The physician that could cure his father was in there – the physician who didn't believe his story, the physician who wouldn't give him the potions. He stopped for a moment, afraid to go near. He also realised this would be the first time he'd been inside one of these modern buildings.

The amazing, almost terrifying sense of surprise came even before they'd passed through the entrance. As they got near the glass doors, the doors slid open. No-one had touched them. It was as if they knew someone was coming. Karl and Cass had to pull him through. "It's just sensors," Ewan said. "There's a magic eye. When it sees people the doors open."

He didn't understand. But when he was inside his head reeled. The room was long, white and spotlessly clean. There were strange frames with words and figures dancing in red. He saw thin tubes on the ceiling that glowed brighter than the brightest furnace. The light was steady, with no flickering. There were chairs by the walls, like church pews, softened with padded cloth. A few people sat on the pews. He saw a kind of glass cage in the corner where two women were working. They had flashing machines in front of them. Cass squeezed his hand. "It's just gadgets," she assured him.

Karl went up to the cage and spoke to one of the women. Then the woman leaned towards a kind of black arm and spoke. "Dr Greaves, your son's here."

There was a little black box in front of her. To Joel's astonishment the box answered. "Thanks Emma, I'm on my way," while, at the far end of the room, a door opened.

A man appeared, dressed in britches with a kind of pale blue smock. He had grizzled, greying hair and wore thin, gold rimmed spectacles, something like the pastor wore. He was tall and big, like a man who enjoyed his food. That didn't seem odd to Joel. A great physician would be able to afford the best food and drink. There was a silver talisman hanging around his neck. The eyes behind the spectacles were gentle. As the man walked towards them he stretched out his hand. "This must be Joel," he said.

His hand was soft, but as Joel took it he was overwhelmed. This was the person who had it in his power to heal his father – or to let him die, if Joel couldn't make him believe his story.

Chapter 12

The doctor led them into a smaller room. There was a smell about it. It wasn't like the smell from Karl or Cass, but it was clean. The desk that stood by the wall was similar to the one in the pastor's study; with a long bed, raised at one end, pushed to the side. Dr Greaves sat on a chair which swivelled so that he could face any way.

There was a kindness in his manner, with none of the roughness of Hab, or the men in the pit. Even Billy Jewell and Walter Bolitho had rough edges – and the pastor – he got quite aroused in the pulpit when he was talking about sin and hell-fire, which he did quite often. Sometimes when Joel had struggled with words in his reading he got very rough.

"Well now," Dr Greaves said. "You've all followed me in, but I need to give Joel a check over. It's not really ethical to have an audience."

Karl grinned. "Patients are allowed a chaperone, aren't they, Dad?"

"True," said Dr Greaves.

"Well," Karl said. "Joel needs three chaperones, OK?"

"I suppose, for the time being, you can stay," Dr Greaves laughed. "I suggest Joel sits by me." He pointed to another of the turning chairs.

The seat was soft, covered with a kind of green fabric. But when he sat down, he had to place his feet firmly on the floor to stop the chair swinging around on its own.

"What are you going to do then?" Karl said. "Have you had a rethink? Have you got stuff for the guy?"

Dr Greaves's frizzled hair was going thin on top. Joel noticed the smooth skin of his head shining through. "All in good time," the doctor said. Then he turned. "Now, Joel, Karl and Cass have told me a lot about you. But how would it be if you tell me something of yourself? You think you came through a time portal – that you live in the eighteenth century, is that right?"

"He doesn't think it, Phil. He *is* from the eighteenth century," Cass said. It surprised him that a girl would address this great physician in such a familiar way, but it didn't seem to bother Dr Greaves. He just held up a hand to stop her talking, and she gave one of her smiles, then put her own hand to her mouth as if to stem the flow of words.

"Is that a miner's smock you're wearing?" Dr Greaves asked.

He nodded.

"Well, tell me about it – and about your family and the work you do."

He found it hard, even though Cass, Karl and Ewan were there. The doctor asked about the injury to his father. When he'd told him about that, the great man said, "Thank you. Is that what you told Karl and Cass?"

"Yes," he said. "And Karl told me you had potions what could cure Father, but then he said you weren't giving them me because you don't believe what I'm saying."

The doctor picked up a pen like the one Cass left for him in the bottle. He started writing. "It's true, it's not as straightforward as Karl makes out."

"It is, Dad," said Karl. "You give him the medicine – tell him how to treat his father. That's no sweat, surely?"

"It's more sweat than you think, Karl, but... we'll sort something." The doctor's face relaxed. He looked at Joel again, adding, "I would like to give you a kind of examination, if you don't mind, Joel, just to put my mind at rest. Would you be happier if the others went out?"

The word 'examination' scared him. "I can't tell what that is, sir – what you'm going to do with me. But I don't want they three to leave me here on my own."

Cass smiled. "He isn't going to hurt you, Joel. He's just going to make sure you're sort of – healthy – isn't that right, Phil?"

He watched the great man pick up a small, silver object, moving his chair. The chair had little wheels so it could ride across the room, but as he moved, Joel shrank back.

"It's all right," the doctor said. "I'm just going to shine this into your eyes." But now Joel's body was as tense as a bowstring. The doctor lifted the object in line with his left eye and there was a blinding light, brighter than the sun. He pulled away in terror.

"It's OK. It's just a torch," the doctor explained. "I shine it into your eyes so I can see what's going on, to make sure your eyes are healthy." He showed him what he was using, pressing a small button so that it lit up, but Joel couldn't help feeling this was the beginnings of some kind of awful torture.

When the doctor shone the torch into his eye again, he kept still. Through his other eye he saw the great man's face, his blue eyes soft, probing. He thought of the Pellar's eyes, the same colour – but hard, glinting with malice, appearing out of slits in gnarled features, her eye sockets puffed with age.

"Hmm hmm," Dr Greaves said. He moved the light to the other eye, peering deeply, as though he was looking into the darkest corners of Joel's soul. Then he turned his head, to peer into his ears.

"Now," he said. "Your mouth. Can you open that for me?"

He shone the torch again. After that he took a small piece wood, using it to press Joel's tongue. It made him want to vomit. "That's OK. I'm almost done," he said. "How are you at reading?"

"The pastor taught me," Joel said. "I learned by reading through the Bible."

"What? All of it?" Dr Greaves exclaimed. "That's more than I've ever done." He took a piece of stiff paper with print on. The print was big at the top, but it got smaller down the page. He pointed to the first sentence. "It's not the Bible," he said, "but can you read a bit of this for me?"

Some of the words weren't familiar. Joel stumbled, sounding them out in the way the pastor had taught him. Again there was a "Hmm hmm," then: "How about this?" He pointed to a sentence in smaller print. Joel struggled with the words he didn't know, but he read others easily. "And then…?" Dr Greaves pointed to the very bottom of the page where the words were tiny. He could make them out though.

"Well, there's nothing wrong with your eyesight, that's for sure," the doctor said. He put the card back and lifted the talisman hanging around his neck. "Now, could you slip off your smock for me, so I can have a listen to your chest and heart?"

Joel had felt his own heart, but someone else listening to it – and the doctor wanted him to take the smock off. It wouldn't be proper.

"I can't do that," he said, glancing at Cass.

"Sure. Cass, it's time to get some coffee in, for five," Dr Greaves said. "Ask Emma. She'll fetch it from the machine. Is white OK for all of you? Bring a few sugars too, just in case."

"I've seen guys with no shirts on before," said Cass, laughing.

"All the same," the doctor said, "if Joel doesn't want it. You're only here at his behest, as chaperones."

With Cass gone, he put the cords leading from the talisman into his ears, turning Joel around, tapping gently on his back.

It amazed Joel. It was nothing like the Pellar's chants and potions. "Now, breathe in," Dr Greaves said. "And hold your breath."

He felt what he guessed was the talisman against his skin. Then the doctor swung him around, doing the same to his chest. After he'd finished, he picked up a box. It had a tube, and a kind of belt which he wrapped around Joel's arm. But when he pressed the box, Joel leapt in terror. The belt was squeezing his arm. No-one was touching it, but it squeezed tighter and tighter. Then it released its grip, while black figures appeared on the box.

The doctor was laughing. "That surprised you, I guess," he said.

"That thing, it be bewitched," Joel gasped.

The great man put the box back on the desk. "It's just something to measure blood pressure." He leaned back in his chair. "Well, that's it. I don't see anything that need concern us – excellent eyesight, your teeth and mouth are healthy. You're in good shape." He wheeled his chair back to the desk. "You can put your smock on now. Karl, go and give Cass a hand with the coffee, there's a good chap."

He began to write again. "There's a small infestation in the hair, but I'll give you something to clear that up."

Ewan laughed, because Joel was looking puzzled. "Head lice, mate. Little blood suckers in your head."

"I got they from the Van when I fetched the Pellar," Joel said. "A man – he was scratching all the way to Penzance."

"We'll give you a lotion," said Dr Greaves.

When Cass and Karl returned they were carrying a metal tray with beakers. The beakers seemed to be made of paper. There was steam rising from them and they were full of a brownish substance. "Have you had coffee before?" Cass asked.

Joel shook his head.

"We'd better put a few sugars in then." She slit open three paper tubes, letting white grains fall into his beaker.

"Now folks. This business of Joel and his father," the doctor said, swivelling around.

"Are you going to give him the drugs?" Cass demanded. "You know – make his dad better?"

But the doctor was still doubtful. "As I said, Cass, it's not that straightforward. It's a matter of ethics."

Karl's face was darkening again. "What can be more ethical than curing a sick man, Dad?"

"That's all very well, Karl. But, you're wanting me to give drugs to a minor – someone none of us knows – some – kid – who could be a vagrant. I mean, if he is – or he's schizoid – or he has some other delusional condition, why would I be giving him dangerous drugs? Anyway, I'm not allowed to dish drugs out to someone with no medical records. Besides, for his part, he doesn't need them – not for himself. Physically he's totally fit. His hair needs a bit of attention, and his teeth don't seem to have seen a toothbrush any time lately, but they're healthy. He obviously hasn't had a lot of sugar in his diet – not until you ladled three packets into his coffee, Cass."

"But he isn't any of those things, Phil. He came up the stope. His dad is dying in the eighteenth century and you could cure him," Cass persisted.

"That's nonsense. It's impossible," said Dr Greaves.

"He's told you," Karl said. "He's told you all about his life. I mean, even I believe the guy."

Dr Greaves wasn't completely finished though. He wanted to know more about mining; about the people in Joel's time. Cass suggested he take a small drink of his coffee, but it had a bitter taste that made him shudder.

"I thought you had coffee in your time, Joel," Dr Greaves said.

"In the towns," said Joel. "There be coffee houses for the mine owners and gentry, sir."

"You can see the guy's genuine, Dad. You've got to do something," Karl said.

The doctor leaned back. "I can't give him the drugs, Karl. But I do have an idea. I'm a GP, and in my practice I see my patients and prescribe medicines to make them better, OK? Say I do that with Joel's father – go and see him – examine him myself – see what's needed, then prescribe the treatment?"

"Phil, that is epic. You mean you'll go through the time portal?" gasped Cass.

"If there is a portal, which I very much doubt," said Dr Greaves. "Whatever else, it'll be an experience."

All of a sudden Joel felt a surge of excitement. "You'm coming to my place to cure Father?" he said.

"It's what I'd like to try, Joel. Provided you're happy to take me."

"I could do that, sir," he said. "And that little light what you shone in my eyes, that would help us see our way. You'd have to tell the people back there you'm some sort of white witch – or a surgeon. They ain't going to believe in no physician coming from after they was dead."

Cass wanted to come to the shaft with them, and Karl said, "Aren't you a bit scared, Dad?"

"No, son," Dr Greaves laughed. "I'm not, because I don't believe we'll be going anywhere. If I do go, though, I'll have to walk two hundred years into the past, so I need to conserve my energy. We'll take the car up to Tehidy and walk from there."

Outside, the doctor chose one of the cars. It was sleek, silver-coloured, much lower in height than a coach, but longer. There were doors on either side, towards the front and back. Cass opened one at the back, signalling for Joel to get in. Then she followed, sliding him along the seat, while Ewan joined them from the other side. Dr Greaves and Karl took the front seats, but Joel was anxious – he'd seen how fast these things went.

The inside was light and airy, and that surprised him. The seats were soft. They weren't opposite each other like the benches in the Van. They all faced forward, and he thought they were more comfortable to sink into than anything he'd ever sat on. The car had a clean smell, too. There wasn't any stench of animal or human bodies, or the smell of fear.

Cass pulled a kind of belt across him, clicking it to a catch. "You have to be strapped in," she said. "That's the law." Then she clipped herself in. So did the others.

"Is it for fear we go too fast?" he said. "For if we do fly out of our seats?"

"That would only happen if we stopped too suddenly," Dr Greaves said.

"And the way you drive, that's highly likely," laughed Karl.

Whatever the doctor did next was followed by a distant, quiet hum, and the car began to move. It was so smooth and gentle, but all Joel's instincts screamed: "You need a horse for a carriage to move." Without being able to stop himself he grabbed at Cass's and Ewan's arms.

They stopped at the entrance. Then, when the road was clear, the car slid out. Houses and hedges slipped by without a shudder or a lurch. It was just the gentle hum, and it felt so odd it made him dizzy. He was still clinging to Cass and Ewan – desperate for the experience to end. They turned down another road, driving past more hedges, then they stopped. He watched Cass undo the straps and open the door. Already they were at the bottom of the hill leading to the stope.

"How was that then, Joel?" Dr Greaves asked.

"It were so smooth and fast, and the softness of they seats – we don't have no seats like that, not even in the king's palace."

The doctor looked at him. There was a slight smile on his face.

But his tone suggested he didn't believe a word Joel was saying. "So, a journey that's a first for you," he said. "Now, if all this is really happening..." Then, gripping a black, leather bag, he added, "Come on. Let's get this show on the road."

Chapter 13

They clambered to the mine's entrance. "How long do you think it'll take, this walk to your home?" the doctor asked.

"It'll take a bit, sir, but it be hard to mark off time."

"There's no point in waiting," Dr Greaves said, looking at Karl. Then he added, "OK, we're off. Whatever comes of this, guys, you'd best leave Joel with me now. Why don't you go to the beach or something?"

They were all looking subdued, and Joel could understand why. It was a big thing, walking into another age. The mine would be busy too. He didn't know how he was going to get the doctor through without being discovered.

Dr Greaves opened his bag, taking out two long, silver cylinders, bigger than the light he'd used in the surgery. "Here. Torches," he said. "Like you suggested. They'll help show us the way." He handed one to Joel, explaining how to operate it. A beam of light as strong as the sun searched out the darkness.

Joel could see the tunnel stretching into the shadows, and for the first time he saw the rock-strewn floor, the huge boulders shouldering between jagged walls, the curtains of spiders' webs spanning the rocks.

"If I lead you through, sir," he said. "I'll look out a route what's easier."

Directing his torch, he moved down the stope, gripping the wall, pushing through the cobwebs. He knew that somewhere ahead there was the warp that would thrust them back to the Pellar and Hab. He was anxious for the doctor's safety. He could hear him stumbling, groping, finding his way over stones and obstacles. For Joel though, there was a fascination, being able to see everything. The deeper he went the more twisted the route became, with turns and crevasses to clamber through.

At last he was at the point where death was all around; the place where there was nothing but himself and the breathless state of timelessness. It was the same today. There were no beating hearts other than his, no breathing bodies, just the cloak of suffocating emptiness. He stopped. It shouldn't be like this. He shouldn't be alone. Then it occurred to him, he hadn't heard Dr Greaves's footsteps for some time. He shouted, but his voice seemed dead. It was as if it had been swallowed by time itself. "Dr Greaves," he called again. "Where you to?" But there was no reply.

"Are you wanting help?" he called.

Still there was nothing.

In panic he turned, scouring the rocks and boulders, peering into fissures, calling the doctor's name. Then he began to walk back, listening, climbing, until, at last, the faint light of the stope's mouth touched the rocks and he saw, silhouetted against the haze, the frame of a tall, portly man, his frizzled hair greying. He seemed to be groping around the walls, searching among the boulders with his torch.

"Dr Greaves," he shouted.

The doctor swung around, staring. "There you are," he said. "What on earth did you do? Where did you go?"

"I was following the stope, sir. There be a place down there what's very strange, as if there ain't no life but mine – where it be only my heart what's beating. When I got there I knowed you wasn't with me. I thought you'd took a fall and got hurt."

The doctor staggered across the boulders, swiping the cobwebs away. "So, where is this passage that you went down?"

Joel shone his torch deep into the chasm. Light searched out the blackness. "Down there, sir. That be where I went."

But Dr Greaves just looked at him. "Do me a favour, Joel," he said. "Go down there again, just a little way, then come back."

"Ain't you coming with me?" he asked, but the doctor shook his head.

"Just go down about twenty paces, then come back."

He set off, clambering over the boulders, going deeper into the stope until he felt he'd gone twenty paces. Then he came back to find Dr Greaves feeling the walls, groping, frowning. When he saw Joel, he had a look of disbelief on his face. "How did you do that?" he said.

"I carried on down the stope, sir, like you told me."

But Dr Greaves shook his head. "No, Joel. That's not what I saw. There isn't any stope. There's just a wall of solid rock and rubble. I don't know how you did it, but you dissolved into the wall." He paused, then nodded, as if to assure himself. "Yes. You dissolved. That's the only way I can describe it. You just faded into the rock."

"But, down that stope," Joel said. He shone his torch into the depths again. "There be a tunnel down there. It do run as far as I can see."

"There is no tunnel," said the doctor. "There's just a massive rock fall. The beams of your torch are bouncing off a solid wall of rock. I thought there might be a hidden fissure, but when you went down the second time I checked. There isn't any gap, just rock and rubble."

But… it wasn't true. He'd gone down a passage. Today, with the torch, he could see the passage clearly. There were obstacles to be climbed. There was no solid wall, though. He shone his torch again, showing Dr Greaves. The light thrust deep into the Earth, turning smoky grey in the distance, beyond the torch's beam. "It be there, the stope. It do run on until I can't see no further," he said.

But Dr Greaves shook his head. "All I can see is a massive rock-fall. It's utterly impenetrable, but you did walk through it. I don't know how you managed it, but you faded into the rock in a way that defies the laws of science. Wherever you go, you must go somewhere. It seems I'm barred, though. If your father's back there, there's no way I can get to him."

"Will he die then?" Joel said. He gazed despairingly into the depths, but Dr Greaves was smiling.

"Not at all. I don't know if this has anything to do with time portals, but you certainly do something. A time portal is as good an explanation as any. It's hard to admit this, Joel, but I'm coming around to believing what you've been telling us. It's OK. Now I know, we'll go back to the surgery. I'll give you medicines, tell you how to treat your father, then you'll go wherever it is you go. I'll give Karl a call – let him know we're still here. I guess they'll have left by now."

They made their way to where the shaft opened to the sunlight, but Karl, Ewan and Cass were still there. They were sitting by the entrance, chatting, soaking up the sun. When they saw Joel and Dr Greaves they staggered to their feet.

"That didn't take long," Cass said. She looked puzzled.

Dr Greaves sat on their tuft of grass. "There wasn't any way through," he said.

"You mean Joel doesn't go through a time warp. You're telling us he's a fake?" said Ewan.

Dr Greaves was still looking stunned. "No, Ewan. Joel's no fake. There was a rock-fall blocking my way, but Joel went through it. He just melted into the rock and disappeared. I don't know where he went, or how he did it, but he goes somewhere. We can't go with him though."

Cass's eyes were wide. "That is awesome," she gasped. She threw her arms around Joel. He liked it when she did these things. He knew his face was burning, but he didn't care.

Karl looked at his dad. "So, if all this is true, Dad, and you can't get back to Joel's father, what are you going to do? You know the guy's genuine. You know he's got a sick father back there. You can't do nothing."

Dr Greaves smiled. "It's still nigh on impossible for me to accept, Karl – the idea of time warps, but we're going to resort to your original suggestion. It isn't ethical, I know, but in the circumstances there's no way that's going to stop me. We'll sort out the drugs. I'll give Joel a crash course, so he can look after his father. Don't fret. Now we know the truth, we'll get Mr Penberthy back on his feet one way or another. We'll nip down the pharmacy. I'll pick up any drugs I haven't got. Then I thought we might pop into Burger King before we make up a kit for him."

Karl laughed, giving his father a push. "Burger King," he said. "He's a doctor, and he stuffs himself with fast food – well, stuffs himself with any kind of food, isn't that right, Dad?"

"A nice bacon double cheeseburger, that's what we'll give Joel," Cass said. "Plus fries and a coke. He's had coke before, down at Ewan's, so he's already getting a taste for that."

As they made their way back to the car, Joel's head was spinning. He would be able to heal his father, and – he was going to get another ride in that car. This time he was determined to enjoy the comfort and the smoothness to the full.

He knew it was eating into an afternoon that should have been spent back in the mine, but he was convinced nobody would notice. They drove past Dr Greaves's surgery, pulling up at a row of shops. One had a green cross outside. In the shop Joel saw rows of free-standing shelves, loaded with neat packages and bottles. "It's a chemist," Cass said. "Phil's getting the medicines for your father."

"Like the apothecaries what we got?" he enquired. "He don't make his own potions like the Pellar, then? I haven't got no coins for paying."

She laughed. "You don't need any. It's all free, on the National Health."

The lady who served them put everything into a crisp, white bag. Then they went to another store with the words 'Burger King' emblazoned on the front. Here Dr Greaves was given a tray loaded with food.

Although Joel had already eaten, the rich smell was tickling his appetite and he was keen to try the bacon double cheeseburger and fries, with coke. There was soft bread enclosing slices of meat and golden slabs of cheese. His teeth sank into it easily. Then there were the fries, crisp and tasty. He'd enjoyed coke before, but there was so much food.

When everything had been eaten, Dr Greaves stood up. "Back to the surgery, then," he said. No-one would have guessed he was a great doctor full of the wisdom of healing. He looked at Joel and winked. "Did you enjoy that, Joel?" Then he rubbed his belly and added, "I'm afraid I did."

"I ate so much I can't move no more," said Joel.

"Oh, I know the feeling," the doctor laughed.

Cass took one of Joel's arms, while Ewan took the other, leading him to the car; but when they reached the surgery he felt the oddest, most exciting of sensations. As he walked towards the door he accepted it would open. He was getting used to this world, the brightly lit rooms, the quiet order, the gadgets, the flashing lights. It was almost as if he was becoming a part of it.

In the surgery Dr Greaves poured the contents of the pharmacy bag onto his desk. "Right," he said. "We'd better get this under way. I'll go through everything with you, Joel, explaining what you have to do, but if you're not sure, stop me. You have to understand exactly what you're doing."

Joel was ready. This great man – everything he did was so different from the Pellar.

There were two potions. One had been put into a small glass bottle. The doctor said it was an antibiotic. It would take the fever and infection away. Inside the bottle were tiny jelly-like eggs, but Joel wasn't so sure about the other potion. There were two shiny discs in a silver tray. Dr Greaves said they were morphine tablets.

Then came the instructions, and what he was told was so amazing he couldn't believe it possible. He'd been certain that, even if his father lived, he'd be crippled for the rest of his life. According to Dr Greaves though, Joel could put the leg back together, just as it had been before the accident. It wouldn't be easy, but he could do it, and he could seal up the gaping wound.

There were no chants, no pot of boiled herbs, just things to be done, and there was a reason for everything. The doctor even told him to get sea water for washing the wound, because the salt had healing properties. Cass wrote everything down. There was so much to remember.

"How close are you to the sea?" the doctor asked.

"It be a rough path, and long, sir. It do take some time," Joel said. "But shifting that bone, that'll hurt Father bad, won't it?"

"Not with the morphine," Dr Greaves assured him. "Morphine will deaden any pain."

He was told he'd need two pieces of wood to support the leg. The doctor called the wood, splints, then there was fabric to bind the wound – with a box of sticky pieces to knit the skin as it healed.

After he' d told him all this, the great man smiled. "There's just one more bit. The grizzly bit. Karl, get coffee in. I think we deserve it."

"Don't tell him anything until I get back," Karl said.

While Karl was fetching the coffee, Dr Greaves read through Cass's notes, pointing out things she'd missed and things she'd written that were confusing. Ewan was pointing things out too. But it wasn't like the pastor when Joel was learning to read and write. It was all done with jokes and teasing. Cass was laughing as much as the other two.

When Karl brought the coffee in, he said, "Now Dad, go on – the grizzly bit."

"There's a shop down the road that sells fishing gear, is that right?" said the doctor.

Karl nodded. "Yeah, it's about half a mile. Why?"

"Maggots," said Doctor Greaves. "We'll pop in to buy a tin of maggots. I want Joel to put a dozen onto the wound before he dresses it."

Cass threw her pen onto the bed. "Phil, that is gross."

"No," laughed the doctor. "Maggots eat the dead and decaying flesh. They'll clean the wound."

"Well, I think it stinks," said Cass, while Karl and Ewan put their hands to their throats, sticking out their tongues, pretending to vomit. They were all laughing.

Joel wanted to laugh too, but, by now, the list of instructions weighed so heavily, all he could do was go over and over, in his head, what had to be done.

Chapter 14

That night it was just Rose waiting for him. He washed and changed by the engine pool, but, when he headed for the mine's wood yard, she couldn't understand.

"Your father, he'm sick," she said. "And you got Mother back home, upset – what with the things she said last night – And all you'm doing is ferreting about, picking up bits of stick. It ain't like you, Joel, boy. You'm always eager to get back to your father."

"I got to straighten his leg," he said. "I need wood what will hold the leg in place."

"Who put that idea in your head?" she gasped. "The pain is going to kill him."

He carried on though, examining pieces lying at random, searching for two straight bits the right length to fit. "I'll make sure Father don't feel no pain," he said.

"If he live, he'm going to be a cripple," she said. "That's what do happen to men down the pit. You can't straighten no leg what have broke like Father's."

There were two pieces lying together. They looked right. He picked them up. "I can, Rose. I learned that today when I got the potions."

"You done it then?" She stiffened, marching away towards the downs. "You met up with this boy what we don't know nothing about?"

"Yes. And I seen his father."

She shook her head. "I wish you'd leave it, Joel. Your mother and me, we know you haven't sold your soul to no devil, but you'm playing with fire."

His father was full of fever when they got back.

"I been worried sick, you going out like that, last night," his mother said. "You know I got a hasty tongue. I didn't mean they things."

He wouldn't answer though. He was still smarting from her words.

"You'm a good boy to your father," she said. "He do know that, and… I know it." When he took the bottle and the silver tray with the shiny discs from his croust bag, though, she breathed sharply. "Where did you come by them things, boy" she demanded. "I never seen nothing like they before."

"They'm the potions," he said. "It be them what will make Father better. The Pellar won't have seen nothing like these."

"You keep they away from the Pellar," she snapped. "If she see you giving your father things like that... and they don't look right."

But nothing any of them could say would stop him. "Fetch me a beaker of water, Obadiah," he said. He opened the bottle, shaking out one of the small pellets, and there was that expression on his father's face again, compliant, trusting. It shot through to Joel's soul. He turned to Rose. "We got to lift him," he said. Then he broke open the thin silver tray, taking out the two discs. "Now, Father, you got to swallow these."

His mother was watching by the fire. But suddenly she went down on her knees, with her hands clasped. "Dear Lord," she whispered. "Preserve Amos, here, from the whiles of the devil. I don't know what my son be doing, Father, nor where he got they potions, but, for the sake of our dear Saviour, save them both from Satan's power, and if it be thy will, return Amos to health."

"It ain't got nothing to do with Satan," Joel said. "It be good people what want to see Father cured." Then he added, "I need a pail. I got to fetch sea water."

"That don't make no sense," his mother snapped. "What's wrong with the water out of our well?"

"It's the salt in the sea water what will heal the wound," he told her. "That be what the doctor said."

She picked up a bucket from by the fire, thrusting it towards him. "Well, I still don't see the sense in it, but nothing the Pellar's doing is helping. You may as well."

The potions and the other things Dr Greaves had given him were still in his croust bag. He didn't believe it would be safe to leave them with his mother or Rose, so he took the bag with him, and as he set out, his mind raced. He'd started the process that would cure Father. The first of the potions were inside him. There were huge tasks ahead though. He knew he had to get hold of his father's bone and move it. It would take all his strength. And how would it be for Father – to have Joel pulling at his bones? Up until now, the slightest movement had brought a groan of pain.

But Dr Greaves had said the little discs would stop him feeling the pain… although, how could he believe that?

Yet, he'd seen the doctor with his gadgets – the silver talisman that could listen to his heart, and that machine that had squeezed his arm; if Dr Greaves said the potions worked, who was he, Joel Penberthy, to doubt him?

He headed west towards Porthtowan, where the path ran away to dunes. The clouds had begun to fracture, their edges were tinged with the silver of a scudding moon. He could make out the splashes of white sand nestled in the darker grass. Shafts of moonlight tipped the swell.

He didn't allow his pail to fill completely. It would weigh him down – or the water would spill, but it was a slow journey back to the cottage. By the time he could see the stuttering light in the window, his arms ached.

He was also beginning to feel more anxious.

He didn't know what to expect, and as he walked through the door he could see things weren't right.

"Hab and the Pellar been here," his mother said. "And I got to say, boy, you're father don't look good."

Father was lying on the bed, very still, as if he was asleep. Even in the light from the tallow candle, Joel could see his skin like wax. His breathing was different too – quick and shallow.

"The Pellar said he'm at death's door," said Rose. "I told Hab I'll stay over, tonight."

"Don't take no notice of the Pellar," he said, although, staring at his father, he was ripped with doubt. Was this how the potions worked? Dr Greaves hadn't explained what they would do. All Joel knew was, the pellets were meant to take away the fever and make the wound heal, while the discs would stop the pain so he could set the bone.

At last he said, "Mother, wake Obadiah. I do need him, and you, Rose."

He could see his mother didn't want any part of it, but she went to where Obadiah was curled, shaking him. "I hope you know what you'm doing, Joel," she said. "I know you to be a good boy, but..." Then she shook Obadiah again. "Wake up, child. Joel do need you for Father."

Obadiah stretched and groaned, staggering across, still full of sleep, while Joel collected some of the things Dr Greaves had given him. There was a bag containing gloves that were thinner than Kelp. He tore the bag open, pulling the gloves on. But his mother was staring. "Where did you get they things?" she demanded. "They don't look like nothing made on this Earth." When he threw the discarded bag onto the fire, it burst into flames, shrivelling to a black blob – and she breathed sharply. "Joel, tell me you'm certain this ain't the devil's work."

He pulled the cover back from his father. "It ain't the devil's work, Mother," he said. Then he turned to Rose and Obadiah, but his voice was shaking. "I want for you to understand what I'm doing – I got to straighten Father's leg. I got to pull the bone back where it belong."

"But the pain, Joel. You can't do that to your father. You should leave him be," said Rose.

"The doctor said the potions won't let him feel no pain," he insisted; although his hands trembled when he fetched the two strips of wood from beside the door.

As he knelt by his father, he was struggling to remember all the instructions Dr Greaves had given him. Rose and Obadiah gripped the leg. His mother had moved to the other side of the room, by the fire. She was sitting, covering her face with her hands.

"I can't look, boy," she said. "How don't you leave your father like he is?"

But Joel didn't answer. Instead he took the broken bone, gripping it with a gloved hand, and he pulled, although with the first pull there wasn't enough strength. He was bracing himself for Father to cry out. Between Rose's and Obadiah's arms he saw his father lift his head, with his eyes half open. But all he did was groan quietly, although that was too much for Mother. "Leave him be," she pleaded.

Now though, Joel had seen enough. His father wasn't feeling the pain. He knew he had to finish the job. With all his strength he tugged again, although this time, with the muscles and sinews fighting him, the bone slipped back.

"Joel, stop. You'm killing him," Rose cried.

But the doctor had told him he could do this. "Hold on to him," he muttered. He gripped the bone for the third time. Then, with all his might, he tugged, twisting until the two edges of the break came together. He held the bone steady, while his father's head lifted once more, then fell back.

"I done it," he whispered. He brushed sweat from his face. But he wasn't finished. "Obadiah, you come down here by me and hold that leg. You stay where you are, Rose, while I fix they wood pieces."

There were tears in Rose's eyes. "Your poor Father," she whispered.

"Hold him steady," Joel said. He placed the two pieces of wood, one on either side of the leg, binding it with a roll of cloth.

Then he put his hand out. "Mother, give me a knife."

"Don't you go cutting him!" she hissed. Her voice was trembling.

"Only the cloth," he said.

But she still kept her head low, so she wouldn't see.

With the cloth cut, he fixed the binding, using pins the doctor had given him. Then, gently, he bathed the wound.

"I got to bring the skin together so it do knit and heal," he explained. He handed Rose the box of sticky pieces. She was staring at him. "They things is going to hold the skin. You stick them on while I put the wound right."

She didn't speak. She just took the strips, laying them across his father's leg.

– And now it was time for the maggots.

But as soon as he opened the tin, Obadiah yelled. “What you doing, Joel? That be foul. Mother, he’m putting maggots on Father.”

Immediately his mother dashed from her chair, grabbing his arm. “Enough, boy. You ain’t putting none of them vile creatures on your father’s flesh.”

“They do eat the bad skin,” he said. “They do keep the gash clean. The doctor told me. You got to trust me, Mother.”

She shuffled back to her chair. “I can’t see how that be right,” she said. “Maggots – they’m filthy things.”

The last task was something called a sterile dressing, a pad the doctor had given him which he bound onto the wound.

He was limp with exhaustion as he sank to the floor. But he’d followed every step of the doctor’s instructions. The job was complete. “Now we got to wait for Father to heal,” he whispered.

“Well, pray God he do,” said his mother. She got out of her chair at last, turning to look. But her only reaction was to sniff. “You done his body up good and tidy, boy, but I can’t help but feel you’m tying up a corpse for the burial.”

Obadiah fetched water so he could dampen Father’s lips, while Joel watched, hoping for some expression in his father’s face. He did move once, and the eyelids flickered. But the eyes were rolling, as if he wasn’t in the same world as the rest of them.

Chapter 15

That night Father's rolling eyes and what his mother had said, haunted him, but Obadiah was warm. In the morning it was hard to drag himself awake.

Mother was sleeping by the fireplace. Rose was watching over Father, although her head had fallen forward. Father lay still, but he wasn't so hot. Joel shook him. When he opened his eyes they were steadier, although they were still heavy, as if his mind hadn't woken with his body. "I got to give you another of they little pellets, Father – the potion," he whispered.

The whispering disturbed his mother. "How is he?" she asked.

"He'm all right. He ain't so hot. He look like he had a good sleep."

"He did," said Rose, waking from her doze. "He hardly moved. That be the first time he've done that since he was hurt last week."

His mother pulled herself to her feet. "First time he've done that since we was wed," she grunted. "He do usually jump about the bed like a beached conger."

As Joel took the pellet from his croust bag, she sniffed. "They things haven't killed him then? I suppose you got to give him another."

He lifted his father's head to feed him the potion. "He'll take some bread and milk now, Mother – to build his strength," he said.

His mother still seemed anxious though, because Father was drifting into sleep again. "Is he all right, Joel?" she asked. "It's like, he ain't with us no more."

It was clear his father wasn't normal. Joel wasn't sure if he'd done the right thing. He still needed Dr Greaves and his wisdom.

As he set out across the downs the thought of Dr Greaves reminded him, the doctor had given a potion for his hair. He'd forgotten to use it. He took the bottle from his bag – just a palm full Dr Greaves had said, and rub it in well.

The smell was overpowering – like the surgery's smell blown up a hundred-fold. It got into his mouth and nostrils, and stayed with him like a cloud. He could understand how something with a smell like this would see off any lurking louse.

There was no sign of Hab at the pithead, although he could sense a tension with the others. It would be hard, working through until croust time. He was thankful, after he'd eaten, to find that the portal to Cass's time still seemed to be open. He felt himself climbing again. Ahead of him would be a bright, cloudless day. He'd be able to tell Dr Greaves about his father.

At the stope's entrance it took a minute for his eyes to adjust. When they did, he saw Cass, waiting on the tufted outcrop. She got up as soon as she saw him, but she was on her own. Her mood seemed odd.

"What happened to they two boys?" he demanded.

"They've gone surfing," she said. "They were desperate to come. But I wouldn't let them. I wanted you for myself today. They only agreed as long as you promised to be here tomorrow. It's like, next week Ewan goes back to London. Me and Karl will be at school. We need you tomorrow. Are you sorry it's only me?"

He wasn't sure how to answer. "I don't think so," he said. "Not if they was *wanting* to be here."

She laughed. "I had to fight them off."

He still couldn't understand. "But, how did you want me without them boys?" he asked.

"Who wouldn't want a guy like you to herself sometimes, Joel Penberthy?" she said. "Besides, my dad and mum want to see you. They phoned Phil last night. He said how you disappeared through a solid wall."

He still couldn't get a grip on the way girls worked in these modern times. In his own world no girl would be as forward as to say she wanted to be alone with a boy. But he was strangely pleased. To be just with Cass – it was Cass who he'd first met in this world. It was Cass who had made him want to come back. He thought he might like it very much to be alone with her.

She was anxious to know about his father. He explained what had happened, but when he told her about the trance-like look, she said she thought that was normal with morphine. But he knew he still needed to talk to Dr Greaves. He wanted to go straight there, although, in this mood, that wasn't what Cass wanted. She said they'd take a bus to her house – go and see her parents, and see Dr Greaves later.

From what he could see, when they'd boarded the bus, it worked like a Van, stopping to pick up and drop passengers as it went. There were rows of seats and a stairway. At the top of the stairs were more seats. But it wasn't like the doctor's car. It rattled like old bones and the smell wasn't good.

It trundled on until Cass informed him their stop was next.

They were nearer Carn Brae now, and she led him along a road to a house with a garden full of grass and flowers. The house was much bigger than most houses in his world.

The hall he was led into was light and clean – with a pleasant perfumed smell. There was a room to their left. But as they entered, he stopped in amazement. This wasn't like any room he knew. Not even the pastor's room in the vicarage could compare with it. There were huge chairs – some longer and crowded with cushions. Rugs lay on a shining wooden floor. Glass globes hung from the ceiling, with fabric shades. There were other globes on stands in corners; again, shaded with cloth mantles. Paintings and likenesses hung on walls and on dressers, and there was a big frame of smoky blackened glass hanging above what looked like a mantelshelf.

For a minute Cass stood, looking at him. Then she put an arm around him and said, "Welcome to my house, Joel Penberthy." She was laughing, but now the laugh was uneasy – as if she wasn't sure of herself. "I've dreamt about this – having you here, just you and me." After that, she turned, and added, "Let's go through to the kitchen. I'll make smoothies."

"But your father and mother," he said. "I thought we was going to see they two, and then the doctor."

She laughed again. "Yeah, sure, but there's no rush is there?"

The room she led him to was packed with more unfamiliar things. He saw a dish full of fruits. He recognised apples, but there were other fruits, large and round, and some like massive yellow claws, bunched, gripping together. Cass took one of the big red and green fruits, cutting away a quarter to reveal a yellow layer of flesh which she pared and chopped. After that she took two claw fingers, peeling their skin, putting everything into a machine. She went to a white cupboard and took a bottle filled with orange liquid, pouring some into the machine. "It all works with electricity," she explained.

When she saw his look of confusion, she added, "You've seen lightning, Yes? Well, lightning's electricity. It's what we use with all our gadgets."

She touched a button and immediately the machine burst into life. The fruit danced, swirling until it had been shaken to a liquid. It made him leap back in alarm. "That's electricity," she laughed.

When the machine had shuddered to a halt she fetched two glass beakers, pouring the liquid out before sitting on a high stool, resting her glass on a table.

He took his drink and joined her. The drink was vivid yellow, thick, flavoured with such unimaginable tastes. "I haven't never tasted nothing like this," he said.

But, as he spoke, she sniffed. "What's wrong with your hair? It's got this weird smell," she said.

"That be the lotion what Dr Greaves gived me to kill they lice. I put it on this morning."

"Then it's time it was washed out," she said. She jumped off her stool. Her eyes were suddenly sparkling. "What if I take your smock and trousers – put them in the washing machine. It won't take long. I'll do them on a fast wash. We can tumble-dry them. Say you have a shower while I do that? I'll give you a twenty-first century make-over."

For the first time since she'd appeared out of the mist last week, he felt uneasy.

"That ain't proper," he said. "If I took them things off, I wouldn't have nothing to cover me."

"It doesn't have to be like that," she replied, laughing, "– not if I give you one of my dad's bathrobes. You can put that on in Dad's and Mum's bedroom. I'll sort the bathroom while you're changing. I can show you how the shower works, then I'll make myself scarce, OK?"

"But, if you wash they things, it will be sunset before they'm dry," he added.

"No. Not with a fast wash and a tumble-dry. They'll be ready in an hour."

"This make-over, then, what you said about. What do that do?"

"I'm going to turn you into a twenty-first century guy," she said. "While your stuff is washing, I'll get you some of my brother's clothes. He's at uni. There'll be stuff around that'll fit you."

"So I do look like Karl and Ewan, you mean?" he asked.

She nodded. "Yeah. You've got it."

He was beginning to catch on to this idea. "I'd like that," he said, "being like Karl and Ewan." It would be like taking another step towards the twenty-first century.

She led him out of the kitchen, climbing a stairway. The stairs had carpet laid, clean, light brown, with a deep pile, deeper than the rugs in the pastor's study. The landing was covered in the same carpet and was bright with sunlight. But, when she pushed open one of the doors that surrounded the landing, he stopped. Beyond the door he saw thick cushions and a soft bedspread lying across a huge bed. There were mattresses piled high, and furniture arranged, fitted to the walls. He could see massive mirrors of flawless glass. Everything was so warm – soft – full of light and air.

"This is Mum's and Dad's room," she said. She went to one of the cupboards, taking out a white robe. "Shift out of those things and slip into this."

But he was overwhelmed. "Your father," he whispered. "He got to be richer than a king to have a room like this."

"Most houses have rooms like this," she said. "Now, I'm off, and I won't come back until you shout for me, OK?"

He nearly stumbled in his hurry to get changed, slipping off his britches and smock, grabbing the robe. He wasn't sure he should be doing this. He needed to see Dr Greaves. He pulled the robe around him, struggling to get his arms into the sleeves.

When Cass came back she was smiling. "You look like a choir boy," she laughed.

Then she took his hand, leading him to another room – nothing like the bedroom. There were troughs, pale green, with bright metal objects attached to them. A tall box-shaped thing stood in the corner. "It's a shower," she told him. "You stand under it to wash." When she pressed a kind of disc, pure water sprayed into a square tray. In a few seconds he saw steam rising like mist. She gave him two bottles of lotion. One was shampoo. She explained the other – shower gel, telling him how to use it. It was like the instructions he'd been given for curing his father. "It be a lot to remember," he said. "I don't think you'll be doing this very often."

But her laugh rang like bells. "Every day, hun."

She kissed him on the cheek, then left.

For a while he wrestled with shampoo and shower gel, following Cass's instructions. When he got used to it, the sensation was so amazing he repeated the whole process. Cass only came back after he'd put the bathrobe on and called her. "I've laid out clothes in Mum's and Dad's room," she said. But before they left she gave him a cylinder that shot jets of spray. The spray had the tree-sap smell of Karl and Ewan.

There were britches in the bedroom, and a smock, similar to the one Karl wore. The clothes were soft to his skin. After he'd dressed he caught an image of himself in one of the mirrors. It made him gasp. He hadn't seen his own reflection since he'd last been at the pastor's. What he saw now was unreal, not like Joel Penberthy at all. The sight entranced him. He couldn't tear himself away.

When Cass called, asking if he was decent, he could hardly make his voice heard. She pushed the door open – then, when she saw him, she stood, staring.

"Wow!" she whispered. "That is so cool, Joel. That is magic."

She led him back to the room with the shower, where she showed him how to scrub his teeth. When he'd finished, his mouth felt cleaner than it had ever felt. He smiled, although Cass's face didn't show a smile now. Her look was softer, almost the look of tenderness. "You are the cutest guy, you know that, don't you?" she said. "Come downstairs and I'll dry your hair."

His body had been bombarded with things that had transformed him. He sat on a long seat, sinking deeply into comfort. This was even softer than the seats in the doctor's car.

When he'd settled, Cass took a machine from a drawer that blew hot air onto him, while she combed and brushed his hair. Her movements were gentle and she whispered, "You are so amazing, Joel – clean and fresh, and..." Her fingers ran through his hair again, down to where it touched his shoulders. "That hair – chestnut brown, and so shiny."

His eyes were closed. He let sensations mingle with a feeling inside that hurt. He was beginning to think, now, it wasn't so important to see Cass's parents or Dr Greaves.

Eventually Cass stood up. She went to a shelf that carried a wooden box. The box had doors. They slid open as she got near, and she fixed a silver disc to the front. But when the doors closed again, the room was filled with the most wondrous sounds – a gentle throb of music, with a girl's voice singing. It was as if Joel was in heaven, listening to the music of an angel. He leapt up. He wasn't expecting it.

"It's Taylor Swift – '*Love Story*'," she told him. "I downloaded it to my phone, but Dad liked it so much he bought the album. How about we sit on the settee for a bit – just listen to it, you and me, together?"

Everything was flooding over him. Sitting in a seat you could sink into beyond comfort, in this amazing room, with the music filling every part of his body. Having this wondrous girl so close – he was full of the most unreal, yet perfect sensations – the perfumes of hedgerows, with Cass putting her arm behind his shoulder. A few days earlier he would have shrunk back; but now he lifted his own arm, hooking it around her, while she lay her head against him. "You are my totally modern, cutest twenty-first century guy, Joel Penberthy," she whispered.

He didn't say anything. He just tightened his grip, letting the unfamiliar feelings fill him. For the moment the harshness of mines and ale houses, the poverty back home, the Pellar and the hostilities, even the worry he felt for his father, slipped away, and he was utterly content.

Chapter 16

At last the music stopped. Cass sat up and sighed. "Your smock and trousers will be done by now," she said. "And we've got to see Mum and Dad."

He was sorry. All this had been so amazing. He knew, when he changed back into his smock, he'd be someone from the past again, a stranger in time.

She led him through the kitchen to a smaller room, where the smock and britches were screwed up behind the window of a white box. When she passed them to him, they were warm – and as dry as a summer's day.

With his miner's clothes back on, they climbed a hill until they came to a pithead.

Some of the outbuildings were like the ones he knew, but he didn't recognise others with their wheels and gantries. He could tell this wasn't the pithead he used. Across the yard from where they stood was a flat-roofed structure, something between a house and the caravans he'd seen down in Ewan's village.

"That's mum's and dad's office," Cass said.

Inside it was furnished similar to the doctor's surgery. At the far end a woman sat at a desk, working with a machine. She got up as they came in. As she smiled, though, he caught his breath. In every feature she was an exact, slightly older version of Cass. She introduced herself as Cass's mother, taking his hand.

"Where's Dad?" Cass asked.

Her mother laughed. "Where do you think? Over in the workshop with his precious wood. He's making doors for the outbuildings."

They crossed to another building, and he could smell the soft aromas of sawdust and sap – the fragrance of seasoned wood. The building they were approaching was packed with machines. From the far end came a searing scream. A man was guiding a plank through a cutting device. He had that concentrated expression on his face. Joel liked the way he steered the wood, tenderly, straight and true. The man looked strong, with an unruly head of brownish hair, cut short, tinged at the sides with grey, but his face had more in common with those Joel knew, weather-worn and used – it was a look that came from the graft of hard work. He wore a short, roughly trimmed beard, and had on a loose, grey smock, with blue britches.

He glanced up as they came in. His eyes were blue, piercing, burning out of sun-smelted features.

He didn't stride out to meet Joel in the way Dr Greaves and Cass's mother had. He just looked from him to Cass, smiling. Then he said, "I'll just get this bit of sawing finished."

He had a rougher accent – more like the accent of a working man. Joel watched as he steered the wood to its end, lifting the cut piece, rubbing a finger over the edge, eyeing it for a true cut. When he'd put it to one side, he looked at Joel again.

"Well, what have we got here then?" he said

Cass seemed totally at ease. "This is Dad, Joel."

"Alistair Blake," the man said. He took Joel's hand. His hold was firm, and Joel made sure his own matched it. That pleased Mr Blake. "I see you got a good grip on you," he said. But when he turned to Cass, there was a questioning edge to his voice. "So this is the lad you reckon to be a mining apprentice who came through a time warp, is that right, Cass?"

"That's what he is, Dad," said Cass. "You know that. I mean, you were on the phone to Phil for an hour last night. He told you what happened."

Mr Blake laughed. "Yes, but, doctors, you know what they're like. Their heads are in the clouds most of the time." He looked at Joel's smock, feeling its hem with his fingers. "I got to say, his dress is authentic. But it's clean, girl, like it's come off the peg somewhere – some theatrical place. And – the guy's a bit well groomed, don't you think? He's wearing deodorant, for goodness' sake."

This wasn't how Joel had imagined the meeting. Cass's face was red. She said, "That's because I took him home and gave him a makeover."

Her mum's reaction to that added to his discomfort.

"You did what?" she said.

"It's OK, Mum. He had one of Dad's bath robes. I put his clothes in the washing machine. Then I showed him how to shower – got him to clean up – wash his hair and stuff."

"That wasn't very sensible, was it?" Mrs Blake snapped. "Taking a young lad home, doing all that. You've only just met the boy, Cass. Anything could have happened."

He began to wish he wasn't here. The way Cass's mother was talking – it seemed he was some kind of bad person.

Cass was looking hurt, too. She said, "Mum. You must know me better than that. I wouldn't have done it if it had been anyone but Joel. He isn't like modern guys. When you get to know him you'll be really sorry for what you said. He wouldn't have let me near the room when he was changing, or when he was in the shower. I mean, when we were with Phil, yesterday, he wouldn't even take off his smock until I'd gone out of the room."

Her mum sighed, but she wasn't ready to step away. "Whatever put it into your head to do it, though, Cass?" she said.

By now his heart was hurting for his poor friend. She looked at her mum. "I just wanted him to know how it felt to be like Karl and Ewan," she said, "give him a sense of our sort of life. I mean, everything here is so different. I let him have some of James's clothes. He loved it, didn't you Joel?"

It was hard for him to speak. "I never wore nothing like they things before, ma'am," he said. "And washing by the engine pool, that don't make you feel clean, not like I was feeling today. And I'd never do nothing to harm your daughter. She do know that." Then he turned to Cass's father because, somehow, he felt less threatened by him. "I was brought up strict, sir. My mother, she be a God-fearing woman, and I know what the pastor do say about wickedness."

Mr Blake smiled, putting a hand on his shoulder. "It's OK, son. I guess Cass got a bit carried away, thinking you're from a different time and all that..."

"He is from a different time," said Cass.

"Phil Greaves seems to think so," her dad said. "But that's a bit hard for me to get my head around. Turning up in a freshly laundered smock didn't help, either. Let's go back to the office. See if you can't rustle up some coffee, being as you're so domesticated."

Cass laughed. "You're such a chauvinist, Dad. It doesn't make me a drudge just because I put Joel's clothes in to wash."

"Well, I'll bet you wouldn't have run to the niceties of coffee."

"I made smoothies," she said.

Suddenly her mother was laughing, too. "You'll be telling us you baked a cake, next."

The colour touching Cass's cheek gave Joel a fluttering feeling. "Give it a rest, Mum," she said.

When they got back to the office, Mr Blake dragged a chair across to one of the desks. "Take a pew, Joel," he said. He sat on the edge of the desk, turning to Cass. "Can you manage that then, Cass – making coffee for four? You fix that and we'll have a chat with Joel."

Cass's mum sat on the desk beside her husband. "Phil Greaves told me about the stope, with you passing through solid rock and all that," Mr Blake said. "But you'll have to accept, it's a big idea for me to take on board."

It wasn't just a big thing for Mr Blake, though. Wherever Joel went, those around him questioned him. He had to tell his story all over again, although, when he explained his own place in the mining process, Cass's father stopped him. "You said you hold the jumping bar while others smite it, is that right?"

He nodded. "We do work together, a couple of apprentices and tributors, my father and me. We work with Billy Jewell, mostly."

"But I was under the impression a tributor held his own jumping bar, turning it in one hand and hitting it with the other," said Mr Blake.

"That would be true in many mines, sir. But Wheal Gwenvor be different. Always it's an apprentice what holds the jumping bar. The others, they do smite it. They put more weight into striking it that way."

"I've got to hand it to you," he said. "You know your stuff. I'm re-opening Wheal Gwenvor. Not for ore though – more as a kind of museum – a tourist attraction. I want people to get a feel for how a mine used to be. After Cass has done the coffee, I'll take you down."

"I seen the engine houses and stacks," said Joel. "And the stamping houses and whim houses. You got a Tommy shop, too – but I ain't familiar with this pithead."

"I don't suppose you would be," said Mr Blake. "Not if it's true, what you're claiming. We're using a shaft that was sunk in the mid-nineteenth century, but it reaches the same levels."

Cups rattled on saucers. Joel knew that sound. The pastor had china cups – although he had never been allowed near them. Cass was bringing them over on a tray, with little edible discs she called biscuits.

He took his cup and saucer tentatively. Priceless, the pastor had told him. Bone china – the crockery of kings. By now he was getting used to the taste of coffee. He liked the biscuits too. They were sweet, easy to bite into.

While they were taking their coffee, he explained about his father and last night, but it was strange, talking to Mr Blake. This was a mine owner – like the Bassets in Tehidy and the Vivian family – powerful people who he wasn't even permitted to look at as they passed, although there wasn't the same awe with Cass's father.

After coffee they crossed to the whim house. He wondered about going into the mine. With a shaft and wooden ladders it would take a long time. But Mr Blake led them into a small box-like room set in the wall. It had a back made of glass, while the front opened to the main room. When he touched something, a lady's voice came from nowhere, announcing: "Doors closing." Then the gaping front of the box shut itself. Instinctively Joel grasped at Cass's arm.

"It's only a lift," she said. As she spoke, though, there was a gentle humming. He could sense a weird motion –

as it they were falling... And they *were* falling. Through the glass at the back he could see the rough surface of a shaft slipping in an upwards direction. "It's taking us down into the mine," Cass said.

Of all the new things he'd come across, this was the most terrifying. They were imprisoned in a cage, falling to the depths of the Earth. He knew he had Cass's arm gripped with the pincer force of a crab. He couldn't speak. He couldn't even blink.

They carried on until a large, squared-off hole appeared through the glass. It was like a window into another shaft. There were men on the other side dressed in strange clothes, with odd looking hats. They seemed to be dead – their faces shining unnaturally, illuminated by some hidden light, and suddenly he breathed sharply. He'd seen creatures like this before – last week, in his vision.

Until now it was the image of the hare and the dog that had stayed with him from that vision. It was the disaster in his own time, but, the wax-like creatures that he'd seen then were here in the twenty-first century. They were in Mr Blake's mine.

The disembodied voice said, "We have stopped for you to see a working man-engine."

"What do you make of that then, Joel?" Mr Blake said. "It's a display I've set up. That's the original shaft back there. We sank a new one to house the lift. That man-engine will be working when the mine opens. We've got wax models going down the shaft. It'll be like the real thing. I managed to lay my hands on a Trevithick steam engine, too. I've made a few adjustments. It's going to operate the man-engine as well as driving the pumps." He said all this proudly, but, for Joel, it could have been a foreign language. Seeing the wax figures was bringing all the horror of his vision back.

"According to you, you wouldn't know what a man-engine is, though, would you – coming from the eighteenth century?" Mr Blake added. "It was used to take the miners into the pit. One platform on the engine would go up while the one opposite went down. All the miners would step across from one to the other. That's the way they got down to the levels in Victorian times."

"We got ladders," Joel said; but his thoughts were everywhere. "We do work at the second level."

"Let's see that then," said Mr Blake. He touched the wall so that Joel could feel the descent again, until the motion began to slow and the hidden voice said, "Second level. Doors opening."

But, as he stepped out, there was another shock. There were no tapers to light the level – just some kind of glass lozenges fixed into the walls. They were shining as bright as a full moon... And he knew... this was the light he'd seen in his vision. There was no tramp of boys with kibbles, no sound of picks or mallets, no rumbling of carts on tracks, just a level with that strange steady light. More of those dead, shining-faced creatures were there, holding picks and shovels. A few trucks stood, with other creatures beside them, frozen in the act of loading the broken gangue.

They explored the level, looking at setts, examining what Cass's dad called 'the exhibits'.

"I've got a section on the third level that's been set up for the eighteenth century," Mr Blake said. "Would you like to take a look at that?"

But when they stepped out at the third level, everything felt wrong. To Joel's right the level veered, plunging deeper into the ground, and when he saw the way it ran to his left, in his mind he was seeing surging floods, with bodies and the wreckage of destruction.

All around there were motionless men and boys made of wax, dressed as he was. And he knew, this was the level he'd seen in his vision. These were the boys he'd seen tossing in the flood last week.

He had to think quickly. "Could I come down here another day, sir? Would that be all right? Today I got to get back to Father, and I got to talk to Dr Greaves. Father – he don't seem right still. But I recognise what be down here."

Mr Blake seemed pleased. "We'll fix something," he said.

When they reached grass Cass's father drove them across to the surgery.

His car was bigger than the doctor's – more like a carriage, although, by now, Joel was getting used to the gentle hum and the smooth speed of passing houses.

He explained the strange changes in his father to Dr Greaves, and the doctor told him much as Cass had – that this was normal with morphine. He assured him that the things he'd done were exactly right. His father would get better. He gave him a new dressing for the wound. After tonight, he told him, if the wound showed signs of healing, he could stop putting dressings on – let the air get in, but he insisted he must carry on with the antibiotics until they'd gone.

With the dressing stowed in Joel's croust bag, Mr Blake took them to the car park by Ewan's camp.

But when they reached it, for a moment, Cass didn't move. Eventually she said, "Dad, could me and Joel go up to the stope on our own – I'll take you when we've said goodbye, OK?"

There was something about the way she said it, and the look her father gave her wasn't like any Joel had seen between a parent and child. It was a look of understanding, with a smile that surprised him – gentle – almost unmanly.

"Sure," he said. "I'll stick around here till you come back." Then he added, "But be careful, love."

Neither Joel nor Cass spoke as they made their way to the stope. They just held hands. When they reached the cave's entrance, Cass looked at him. "You *will* come tomorrow, won't you?" she said.

He nodded. Suddenly he felt choked. He was afraid of what might happen if he spoke.

She kissed him on the cheek – then, gripping his head, she kissed him again, right on the lips – and he tensed.

He understood though – She was telling him she liked him. No girl that he knew in his own time would show feelings so openly, although, in Cass's world, it seemed right. He knew he wanted her to like him, and it was strangely exciting – being kissed like that.

His heart was racing when she released him. He staggered to the head of the stope. But, before he made it into the darkness, he turned – just to take one last look at this amazing girl. She was standing in the entrance, shaped against the glittering daylight of her time. Then something changed. She remained in his vision, while the jagged outlines of the stope's entrance faded. Instead, he saw the whole hill, gorse bushes in yellow bloom, the white of May – And... dashing in front of Cass was the form of the white hare, followed by the black dog.

Immediately, he knew – this hare and this dog were running in Cass's time, the time of the wax figures and the levels he'd just seen in Mr Blake's mine.

He could hardly breathe.

Slowly the vision faded, so he saw just the stope's entrance. Cass wasn't there now. He guessed she'd gone to fetch her father. But he'd seen the portents again, this time where Cass's father had his mine. Cass, Karl and Dr Greaves had done so much for him – their kindness – the way they were helping save his father's life… Now he believed they, too, were facing some sort of catastrophe. He couldn't let that happen.

It was a long time before he turned, stumbling towards the darkness and the grim realities of his own world.

Chapter 17

The rain was sheeting across the moors as he stumbled through to the cottage with Rose. Hab was already there– with the Pellar. She was bending over Father. Joel made out her face in the spasmodic light – walnut wrinkled, her mouth twisting out the words of her mindless chants, her skimpy grey hair shadowing her features, her body gaunt with age. Her image contrasted with Dr Greaves and his kind intelligence, working with a knowledge of illness and its remedies in his clean, airy surgery.

He looked around; at the fire feeding on peat and logs, the clouds of choking fumes blowing back down the chimney. There was the dark corner where they slept, and the sparse furnishings, ground down with age and dirt. The doors didn't fit – the windows were gaping. He looked at the trivet with its pot steaming – the same old soup, day in and day out.

Now he knew something different; he knew the clean spacious light, the soft clothes, the settees where you sank into luxury, with showers and gels, food that came from heaven, and the music of angels.

But it was his father lying there. It was his family who lived in this penury. As soon as the Pellar had finished he would go to Father. He knew the doctor's potions worked. He could see Father, more at peace.

"I'll fight on, boy," the Pellar said. She struggled to her feet. "Now I've seen what you'm doing, I'll put a stop to your sorcery."

He didn't answer. All he said was: "Obadiah, fetch over some water."

He took the bottle from his croust bag – just one small, egg-shaped jelly to speed his father's recovery.

But, straight away, Hab made a grab. "What you got there? What you fetching from that bag, boy? You give they poisons to me. You ain't doing no more harm to Father."

Immediately, Joel pulled away, but, as he did, he heard his father's voice, firm and strong.

"You leave the boy be, Habakkuk Penberthy. He ain't doing nothing but good."

It was the first time he'd heard his father speak since the accident.

But the Pellar swung around with her eyes flaming. "Nothing but good?" she snarled. "There be black magic running amuck in this house, old man." She made her arms form a cross, muttering some weird chant, but Father's eyes were on Hab.

Years of enforced obedience made him shrink back, so that Joel was able to kneel beside his father. "Just one of they little pellets like what you took this morning," he said. "Then another before you go to sleep. I got to look at that leg, too."

He pulled the blanket away. The wound was so much better. Quickly he gathered the old maggots into a cloth. There were more in his croust bag, along with the new dressing, but when he'd washed the wound, as he placed first fresh maggot on his father's leg, Hab leapt at him again.

In one swoop he snatched the tin.

"What's he doing?" the Pellar demanded.

"He'm putting maggots on Father. He've got hundreds here, look, in this box!"

"Servants of Beelzebub," the Pellar hissed. Then, with a snarl, she hurled the tin onto the fire. "They things came from Hell, and that's where they'm going back."

Immediately Hab grabbed Rose by the shoulder. “You get out from under this roof right now, girl,” he said. “Take the Pellar over to our place.” He turned to his mother. “That varmint be putting maggots on Father. The servants of Beelzebub the Pellar do say. That ain’t right. I ain’t staying here to see such devilry.”

He slammed the door, while the Pellar stopped her ritual chant and turned to Rose. “You heard what the boy said,” she hissed. “No good-living Christian can bide under this roof. But you’ll have to carry that pot and they potions. They’m too much for me.”

With the Pellar and Rose gone, no-one said anything for a long time. He could see his mother was troubled. In the end, though, she shook her head. “I can’t see it, boy. How is it black deeds if your father be getting better?”

“It’s all right, Mother,” he said. “That Pellar, she’m a bad woman.”

He was still kneeling by his father. He’d rescued a handful of maggots before Hab took the tin. Then, as he put them on the wound with the dressing, he caught that look again – the look of trust and gratitude on his father’s face.

It was well into the evening when Hab came back. Obadiah was asleep. His mother dozed by the fire and Joel was ready to give Father the third pellet.

Quietly, so as not to disturb the others, he poured water, crossing to his croust bag.

But as he lifted the bag, he heard noises across the downs – a chanting. There was a rash of lights – tapers burning – the slurred sound of shouting. He didn’t work out what it was immediately, but when he did, he shot the door’s bolt, while his mother leapt from her chair. “What’s that row?” she demanded.

"A crowd coming, Mother, with lit tapers. It be a rabble. They'm sounding the worse for the beer."

She crossed to the window, wiping the grime away. "They'm heading this way," she muttered. "And what is it they'm shouting?"

Joel guessed what had happened. Hab had gone to the ale house, and he wasn't one to keep his mouth shut. The mob were already aware of what the Pellar was saying. Now they knew about the potions and the maggots. Hab would have stirred up feelings. The rabble was out for blood. He listened again. Along with the heavy tramp of feet he heard his name. "Joel Penberthy," and other names – "Beelzebub," "Satan," while Hab's voice shouted above the rest, "Come out here, runt."

His mother's face hardened. "It be time you got going, boy," she said. "That bunch of ale soused idiots isn't on no social visit. You go out the back. I'll say you ain't here."

"I can't leave you, Mother," he said. "And there's Father and Obadiah. That lot got brains what be pickled. They don't know what they'm about. I got to face them."

But his mother didn't move from the window. "The likes of your brother and that dolt Sam Eustice with his band of idiots ain't no bother to me, boy. As for Habakkuk – I'll take a stick to him. You needn't fret about me nor your father, nor Obadiah."

He didn't want to go though. Whatever else, he had to give Father the potion. Lifting him from sleep he whispered, "Take this, Father. And don't you worry about that bunch of fools outside. There ain't nobody going to hurt you."

His father was only half awake. He swallowed the capsule. Then he fell back onto the straw. But the tramping feet and the cries were getting nearer. Through the window he could see the flickering of orange torch light tinting the soaked branches of trees and shrubs.

"Come on out," he heard.

Then, led by Hab, the shouts changed to one continuous chant. "'Joel Penberthy', 'Joel Penberthy'."

By now Obadiah was awake. He'd run to Mother, but Joel still didn't move.

At last his mother grabbed his croust bag, pushing him to the other side of the room. "I ain't having the likes of Sam Eustice nor Hab Penberthy coming nowhere near you, boy," she said. "You get out the back. Go across to Billy Jewell's. He'll give you shelter. You leave that bunch to me. I'll serve them up a thought or two they won't forget in a long time – and I will… I'll take the stick to Habakkuk. It's time he learnt his place."

He didn't have any choice. She bundled him through the back door. The bolts shot and he was left with only two options. Either he went around the front to face the mob, or he made it to Billy's. He could already hear his mother shouting above the chants. Within seconds the rabble's calls had simmered to a murmur. But he felt ashamed. With Father sick, his place was in the cottage protecting his family.

It was only with reluctance that he made his way across the downs. He could still hear mutterings, but it was his mother's voice that rode every other sound.

There was no light when he got to Billy's. The sound of his knock rattled in a void, but then – "Who's there?"

"It be me, Mr Jewell – Joel Penberthy."

A flint struck, followed by a flutter of orange light. "Is it your father, boy? Have he been took worse?"

Billy was standing, candle in hand, in the doorway.

Joel shook his head. "Mother sent me. I come over to hide out. We got a mob up our place from the ale house. They was after me. They'm thinking I'm doing the devil's magic on Father."

Billy guided him to a chair by the fire. "Sit yourself there, boy. I've heard rumours."

"I ain't going to let Father die, though," Joel said. "And I found people with potions what's making him better."

By now Mary Jewell was up, standing by the trivet. "How did you find these people, Joel?" she asked.

"I can't tell you, Mrs Jewell," he said. "There ain't nobody in this County what would believe me. But I found them. The potions what they gived me is in my croust bag." He took out the bottle with the jelly-like pellets, showing them what was left of the medicines Dr Greaves had given him.

"They things look very strange. I can't say I've ever seen the like before," Billy said.

Mary was turning over the packet of sticky material. She shook her head. "Me neither. They don't look like nothing from around these parts."

"That be why I can't tell nobody," he said. "They do come from these parts… but… the Pellar and Hab, they'm spreading it about that I'm in with Satan. I think that mob had it in mind to kill me."

"You can stay with we for as long as you want, son," Billy said, taking his hand. "But you'll need to keep low for a bit. It won't do you no good going down the pit, not while all this be going on. I'll have a word with the underground cap'm, see what we can do, but while they men are in this mood, you got to keep clear of them."

Joel knew he was right, but it wouldn't be easy.

That night he took a rug to settle by the door. Emily, Billy's daughter, was the same age as he was. They were both ripe for the marriage bed. It wasn't right for him to sleep any closer. Through the night, though, as he tried to sleep, he was weighed down. There was Father. And there was Hab's mob, out for his blood.... Now there was Cass, and Mr Blake's mine – the vision he'd seen, the warnings. He knew he had to do something about that...

Billy and Mary left for the mine along with Emily well before dawn. After they'd gone Joel waited for the first hints of daylight. He watched the morning creep across the clouds, heavy, joyless, but he didn't move from the cottage until the last worker had passed. He needed to get back to Father, though, to give him the potion. He knew he would have to follow a route using the cover of hedges.

He was half afraid he'd find his parents' cottage torched. It was a relief to see it still standing, squat in its field, white and unscathed.

Father was sitting up, with Mother at the table building tomorrow's pasties. Later she would take them to the bake house in Illogan. There was no sign of Obadiah. Joel guessed he'd gone to the stream for trout.

His mother looked up as he came in. "You got clear last night then? You got to Billy Jewell's?"

He nodded. "He said I can stay for as long as I want, but he don't think I should go down the pit, not till all this have died down. You was my main worry, Mother. Was you all right?"

"A drunken rabble ain't no threat to me, boy," she grunted. "I gave it to them straight. I told that boy, Habakkuk, he was heading for a good hiding – and I did, I took the stick with me. They soon sloped off when I said you wasn't here. I ain't convinced it's the last we'll see of them though, not when the ale start talking again. You'm best off over Billy Jewell's."

He looked at his father. "He'm getting better, Mother. I come back to give him the potion."

"He took a drop of soup this morning," his mother said. "I'm doing him a pasty for later. But – they potions, boy. I been thinking. Are you sure it be them what's doing this for Father? It could be the Pellar. She do keep up with her potions and chants."

Suddenly his father shifted. Joel heard his voice again, strong and certain. "What are you talking about, Mother? That woman do curse me to hell every time she pour her filthy muck down my throat. She don't want me better. It be Joel, here. It have always been Joel, from the minute he found me down the pit. He've nursed me like a woman. He've fought against that witch."

His mother dropped the pasty, grabbing his hand. "Don't go upsetting yourself, Amos," she said. "I weren't thinking. 'Course it be Joel. He'm a good boy. But they potions, I can't see that they be fitty."

His father pulled away. "Good ain't the half of it. He turned Heaven and Earth upside down to help me. It was him what kept me going. All through last week he stood by me, and I knew it from the first. I knew it would be Joel what would see me through."

By now Joel could feel an ache in his throat. It was twisting inside him so that he couldn't help himself. Suddenly he dashed over to his father, dropping down beside him, hugging him as they did in Cass's world, and he was sobbing.

His father patted him like a child. "There, boy," he said. "Don't you fret yourself. Your father have always trusted you. You been a good boy to me. I won't never forget that."

But, even as the poison of the last days melted from his soul, he turned for the door. He looked out across the moorlands. All the austerity and hardship of his birthright was out there, and there was his mother and his father... But there was Cass, and her father's mine – and he was torn as he'd never been.

Chapter 18

"Are you going out?" his mother demanded.

He picked up his croust bag. "I'll be back later. I got to give Father the potion tonight and I got to change that dressing on his leg."

"Well, where you going?"

"Just out," he said. "It ain't safe staying here. If Hab's mob is after me, they'm going to look here first."

He knew this wasn't the true reason why he was going, but his brain was churning.

"I done up a pasty for you yesterday," she said. "Take it with you, and be careful." She opened the bag, pushing the pasty in. "It be a mess, all this. But what do hurt me most is, Habakkuk – my own son, he'm the cause of it."

"It be true, boy," said his father. "It break my heart, thinking what that boy's doing."

A restless force drove Joel though. He pulled the croust bag onto his shoulder, turning for the door. "Look after him, Mother. And make up a pasty for him. That'll be good. I'll get back when it be dark."

Heavy shadows swept across the downs. He headed towards the coast, but he knew, today, he was going to take massive risks.

He had to go to the mine. He couldn't see another disaster. He couldn't see Cass's family hurt. And there was the other thing. He'd promised Cass and the boys he'd come back today. He was desperate to be with his friends. He knew it was madness. He'd given up on a day's work to keep clear of the mine and its hostility, yet, the mine was his only route to Cass's world.

He didn't want to get there too early. The stope only seemed to reveal itself at croust time. This was one reason for heading to the coast. It took longer. It was safer; but the vast stretch of sea with its expanse of grey-green was also a place for thinking. There was a restlessness about it on moody days – and today that matched his own mood.

The fresh saltiness of spray touched his face as he stood, letting the wind play through his hair. He was thinking about what lay ahead – the vision – the threat of disaster. He was certain something was going to happen in the third level of Mr Blake's mine. He'd had that feeling when he was there yesterday. He also believed there'd be a connection between the two third levels; the new one and the one already flooded. In his first vision he'd seen water filling the new level. That water had to have come from somewhere, and he believed it would have come from the old, flooded level. Yet, how could he find what would make the disaster happen? He had to see plans of his own mine – see where the flooded level ran. He thought the plans would be in the mine office, and he knew, to see them, he'd need to break in like a common criminal.

Walking on, he listened to the whispering of the sea. He was standing high on an outcrop now. The rugged lines of coast stretched away like ramparts, with white foam lacing the rocks, and the surging grey stretching to oblivion. At last he reached Porthtowan, but his mind was still in chaos. Restlessly he kicked at the sand, struggling with his feelings. Finally he turned towards the moors, approaching the miners' cottages and the buildings clustered around ale houses and dram shops.

He kept as well hidden as he could. If he was discovered...

He was eager, now, to make it to the mine and its shaft. Then he would be away from daylight, although he would still have to run the gauntlet. His only protection in the mine would be the lack of light.

All around him clouds dropped like weighted bags. They began seeping a thin, penetrating drizzle, but now he could smell the sweet oil lubricating the beam engine, along with the heavy fumes of smoke and sulphur. He could hear the stamp of bal maidens and grass-level men breaking the gangue. There was the run of water in the troughs and adits – the shuffling of ore on vanning shovels.

He crept around the back of the outbuildings so he could get to the engine pool. He had to change into his smock. If he was seen wearing ordinary clothes in the mine there would be no way he could conceal himself. Breathing deeply, he slipped the smock over his head. It still held the freshness of Cass's washing – and that excited him. Finally he sidled towards the shaft, hiding behind buildings, darting through the yard so he could get to the back of the dressing floor and across to the engine house.

Now, though, above the hiss-boom of the beam, he heard the crunch of footsteps. Immediately he froze. There was a voice. "Joel – Joel Penberthy, is that you?" He didn't know whether to dash for the shaft or turn. The voice was low, almost a whisper – a bal maiden.

When he looked, he saw Rose, her face clouded with alarm. "What you doing here?" she whispered. She steered him behind one of the sheds. "You ought to be up Father's – keeping clear of this place."

"I couldn't, Rose. I got to see they people again."

She stared at him. "Have they got some kind of hold over you? Can't you see the danger, boy? They was hell-bent on taking you last night. Hab told me – and I can see why. This cure – they potions what you'm giving Father. I seen you. It be like, you'm bewitched. You do things what no-one else could do, and the things you use – they haven't got no place on Earth."

He looked at her. "You ain't believing what they do say, are you, Rose – that I'm the devil's child?"

"Sometimes I don't know what to think," she said. "Hab and the Pellar, they'm telling that Father be getting better, but they'm saying it's the Pellar's potions and white magic. They be whipping up feelings against you, boy, putting it about that they got to fight the blackness of your deeds. It's giving them reason enough to finish you. And these people what you won't talk about – what kind of hold have they got on you, coming down here in the middle of the day?"

It wasn't safe around the back of the outbuildings. He was desperate to find cover in the shaft. "You got to believe me, Rose," he said. "The Pellar ain't doing nothing for Father. It's them potions what they people is giving me, that's what's doing it. They'm good people. I wish I could tell you how it is I get to them, and who they are."

"Well, why don't you?"

"Because all this – it be bigger than your head could take. I can't hardly believe it. Neither can they – not the people what's curing Father."

Rose shook her head. "Well it don't make no sense. Your mother and me, we know you ain't bad. It's just – the Pellar – and Hab. I never seen such hate. It do hurt me to say this, boy – Hab being your brother and my husband, but they'm thinking to destroy you. It don't do to take chances with them."

He knew it was true, but still… he couldn't tear himself from the stope.

He moved away, heading for the shaft.

Then, rung by wooden rung, he descended.

With every step the heat grew. There were hints of hell-fire. The thickness of the air carried smells – sea-salted earth and stone, the mustiness of an atmosphere never touched by sunlight – and that stench again, the sulphurous smell that had sent fear through him exactly one week ago – the reek of gunpowder.

As he reached the second level he could hear men – the steady rhythm of hammer blows and picks, the rumble of trucks, the sound of kibbles sliding their loads into the shafts. The air was bad. Boys were kneeling over candles, fanning them. A truck trundled by, making him seek out the deepest shadows. He was a long way down the level; almost at the place where Mr. Blake had his lift. Then one of the tributors noticed him. It was too dark for him to be recognised, but the man called: "Here, boy. Give us a hand. Fan this candle. We'm short on boys. We can't hardly see."

He pretended not to hear, moving away, back towards the shaft, but the man threw down his mallet. He staggered out of the sett and Joel heard the voice again. "Boy. Haven't you go no ears? I said come and fan this candle."

He was in a panic now, and he struggled to run, groping over rocks, labouring where the level narrowed and twisted.

Others stopped work.

Then a boy on one of the trucks yelled: "That be Joel Penberthy."

Someone cursed, but he ran on, blindly pushing past men and boys.

"Get the varmint," the tributor called. "He'm up to no good. I'll lay odds."

By now the boy on the truck had joined the chase. He could hear others – feet pounding, heavy breathing, men gasping.

"Help me, Bucca," he whispered. "Get me safe."

His eyes were shut, his lungs bursting, his heart thumping, he could feel his back, his neck, his chest, all on fire. With every gasping breath there was less good air.

And now he was falling, losing his senses. The shouting was fading. He could hear less of that terrifying footfall, until…

Silence, a waft of sea-salt – a cold disturbance touching his face.

His feet could barely take another step, and he staggered, breathless, gripping the wall. But now there was no sound – no shouting – no pursuing footsteps – no heartbeat except his own – nothing ahead of him or behind. Slowly, he opened his eyes. Beyond the darkness he could see the steady silver glow of Cass's world… and the baying rabble had gone.

Chapter 19

His friends were sitting on the outcrop, waiting. Cass ran towards him as soon as she saw him, while Ewan followed, explaining, “We’re off down to Portreath. My lot have gone to St Ives. We’ll kit you out back in the caravan. We’re going to teach you surfing.”

“I ain’t working in the mine today, so I can bide here till late,” he told them. But he wasn’t free of the shock. He’d been so near getting caught. “It ain’t safe, going back,” he added. “I got to wait till the tributors and tut workers be gone home.”

“Why?” Ewan asked.

“It’s trouble back there. They don’t like the potions what I gived to Father. They’m saying it be the black arts. We had a mob up the cottage last night, from the ale house. I had to get away.”

“That is gross,” said Karl. “What planet are your lot on?”

“They ain’t like you, that’s certain. Today I went down the mine to get here, but they seen me and set up a chase.”

As he said it, though, he realised just what had happened back there. The men would have watched him melt into the rock, just as Dr Greaves had done. By this evening it would be the talk in every cottage and ale house.

“Can’t you just stay here?” said Cass. “Say they’d killed you?”

“I got friends,” he said. “Walter Bolitho, the underground cap’m – and Billy Jewell. It be him what’s giving me sanctuary.”

“But it’s so dangerous,” Cass said. “What would we do if anything happened to you. Say if you didn’t turn up one day – how would we know? It would be in our heads they'd murdered you."

"I shall always come back," he said. "I got to keep alive for Father, and to be here with you." He found it hard to speak.

"If you didn't show, though," she persisted. "We'd be living with that for the rest of our lives."

"It won't happen," said Karl.

Joel put an arm around her. He knew he could do that now. "I gived you my word," he said. "I ain't in no danger, not with the underground cap'm looking out for me. I just got to keep clear of they people what mean me harm, that's all – till Father be cured… and then..." But he couldn't get to grips with what lay beyond his father's recovery.

"Are you certain?" Cass persisted. She brushed tears from her eyes.

"I won't never let nothing happen to me," he promised. They were climbing the hill towards Ewan's caravan now, but he knew he was saying it to give Cass comfort. He didn't really have so much confidence in his own future.

None of them spoke much after that, until they reached the caravan. Then the mood lightened. Four boards stood under the awning, like the one he'd seen Ewan carrying when he'd first met him.

"I've dug out a pair of jeans and a T-shirt for you," Ewan said. "We can catch the bus down to Portreath." He grinned. "I figured you'd want to be a bit private for changing, Yeah? You can do it inside – I mean, you don't want Cass's snooping eyes on you, do you?"

He guided him into the caravan. But what Joel saw inside was beyond belief. It was a compact home on wheels, with wooden cupboards, long cushioned couches, a table, a carpeted floor, sinks, taps – other devices – smaller than his father's cottage, but with so much more in it.

"This be some place," he gasped. "I could live in here forever."

"Dad's dead serious about it," Ewan said, smiling. "He belongs to the Caravan Club."

He picked up a pair of short britches. "Put these on. They're like boxers, for wearing in the sea. Then put the jeans and T-shirt on. I looked out a pair of trainers." He glanced at Joel's shoes. "You're about my size, yeah? Leave your own stuff on the seat for when we get back."

When Joel came out of the caravan, Karl grinned.

"That's real cool," he said.

Cass fumbled in a bag slung across her shoulder. "He needs a comb, though."

She was quicker today, although there was still a softness in her look. When she'd finished she said, "Now he's well smart."

"Yeah, stunning," said Ewan. He gave him one of the surf boards and added, "Let's go. There's a bus, like, due in five minutes?"

This time Joel felt the transformation was complete. As they made their way back down the hill he was carrying a board just as he'd seen Ewan do last week. He was wearing modern clothes. No one would know he wasn't part of this world.

He'd been to Portreath before, when he'd helped with the moyles – mules slung with panniers taking ore to the harbour – but what he saw from the bus now wasn't what he remembered. Now there were neat rows of white cottages with brightly painted doors and windows, clustered around roads leading off the main thoroughfare. To his left were beautiful houses set in the emerald cliff. Shops and other buildings stood at the edge of the main road, with rows of cars glinting in a huge yard just in front of the beach.

The walkways were full of people dressed in bright clothes, some wearing dark spectacles against the sun, some with boards like his own. There were children with small pails and shovels, people carrying bags and packs. The air was brisk, tinged with the tang of seaweed and salt, and everywhere had a feeling of joy and happiness. But, when Joel reached the beach, he stopped. He grabbed Ewan, propelling him away.

"What is it?" Ewan asked.

"They people," he whispered. "Down on that sand. They don't hardly have no clothes on, men and boys, and…" His eyes were wide. "And they maids, they got arms and legs showing – and them shoulders."

"It's the beach," Ewan laughed. "Sunbathing and swimming, it's what we do."

"But..." Joel said. "That ain't right, men and maids together doing that. I can't go down there."

By this time Cass and Karl had drifted up.

"It's OK, Joel," Cass said. She was laughing too. "I told you. People nowadays, they're like – liberated. It's what Ewan said – what we do – swimming, surfing, kids playing."

Ewan put an arm around him. "Look, mate," he said. "You want to be like us, yeah? This is how we are. It's all normal for us."

"You mean, it be all right for Cass to see me like they men down there?"

"Yeah, sure," said Cass.

"But I'm scared stiff," he said.

"You're weird, mate," laughed Karl. "You know that, don't you? I mean, last night you had to fight off a mob of drunks hell bent on killing you, and you're scared about stripping off on a beach. Come on, man. Get down there."

"I know I got to, if I want to be like you."

He looked at the hundreds of bodies and took a deep breath. He'd set his mind. He would do it. Today he was in the twenty-first century. Before his determination could dissipate, he marched onto the sand, but everything he'd been taught screamed it wasn't right to be within touching distance of so many scantily clad females; although none of the people around seemed to share his concerns. Some read. Others had strange mechanisms clipped over their ears. They were gently rocking their heads. Some just lay, soaking up the sun. Down at the edge of the water, people played in the waves and swam. There were those in black, skin-hugging suits, using the surf boards. Some were even trying to stand as they rode the waves, generating peals of laughter when they fell over.

But when Cass found an empty patch on the sand, and Ewan laid out their towels, his intentions were completely blown apart. Without a second thought, Karl and Ewan slipped off their britches and T-shirts. They kicked off their shoes. Cass did the same. Bare legs, arms and shoulders reeled in his vision. In panic he turned, staring at the horizon.

Ewan laughed. "Joel, mate. You really need to chill. You won't have any fun if you stand there like an Antony Gormley statue for the rest of the day. Now, get those jeans and T-shirt off, or Cass will do it for you."

He knew his friend was teasing, but... He wanted more than anything to be part of their world. He closed his eyes. Then, in a single movement, he tore off the T-shirt and jeans, kicking off his shoes. He still had his eyes closed, but his friends were cheering. He heard Cass say, "Wow, Joel."

When he opened his eyes, they were all standing near him, and it wasn't only Cass who was staring. Ewan said,

"That is one mean body, mate. You've got muscles where I didn't know muscles existed."

Karl produced a bottle, handing it to him. "You'll need to put this on though. Rub it all over, or you'll burn like a lobster."

"Like you did with the shower gel yesterday," Cass said.

The boys looked at her, and she laughed. "I gave him a makeover. He took a shower."

They didn't make judgements like Mrs Blake. Ewan just said, "Cool."

Joel smeared lotion on his front, then his arms and legs, but there were parts of his back he couldn't reach.

"Let me," Ewan said. He took the bottle, gently working the lotion in. His movements had a softness that Joel felt wasn't manly, but… he liked what was happening. Boys and men weren't ashamed to be gentle with each other. That was a good thing.

When Ewan had done, they passed the bottle back to Karl, while Ewan said, "Now, the sea. Let's have a dip first, OK?"

Before he'd finished speaking he was charging down the beach, with Cass and Karl following. For a moment Joel stayed where he was. Then he made a rush to follow, throwing himself into the biting water, splashing, leaping, plunging up to his arms and shoulders, rolling with the waves. The others tumbled on top of him, while the happiness – the joy that filled him was like nothing he'd ever felt.

After they'd been in the water for a while, Ewan suggested surf boards so they could teach him to body-surf.

And he could do it.

He let the board ride the waves. He rolled when it rolled, laughing and shouting with the thrill of it. Karl and Ewan tried standing on their boards, but, to Cass's and Joel's delight, they toppled off. Ewan claimed the surf wasn't up so it wasn't easy to stay upright.

Eventually they went back to lie out on towels, letting the warmth of the sun soak into their skin. Karl made him put on more lotion and... Already he'd forgotten he was almost stripped bare in the company of hundreds of scantily clad women. Already he was comfortable with the sight of his three friends.

There was the murmur of chat, the shouts of laughter, the sound of distant waves. He didn't feel any urgency – no drive to combat the hardships of life, no need to talk; just the occasional comment or quip, until Ewan sat up.

"I don't know about you guys, but I'm starving," he said. "Say we get fish and chips?"

"What about you, Joel?" Cass asked. "Are you hungry?"

He was. He hadn't eaten his pasty. His croust bag was back at the caravan. "I didn't have nothing to eat today," he said.

"Well, that settles it," said Ewan.

They left their britches, slipping on shoes and T-shirts, taking a route through the yard until they came to a kind of courtyard beyond the cars where a white building stood. Two young men and a girl plied their trade at a counter. It reminded Joel of Burger King.

People waited beside tables or sat on a wall outside. Every now and again one of the men or the girl would shout a number and hand out white boxes.

"Coke for everyone?" Ewan asked. He stood talking to one of the men. There was a brief discussion with Karl about paying, but Ewan insisted they were his guests.

Back on the beach he explored his box. There was cooked fish encased in a strange pastry… with potatoes, similar to the fries at Burger King.

He noticed how the others ate, using just their fingers, so he pulled a piece of the encased fish away. This food was so satisfying. To be here, eating with his dearest friends, surrounded by hundreds of people, with the gentle breeze off the sea and the sound of the waves – it was as near paradise as he'd ever been.

While they ate, the tide sank down the beach. Ewan explained about caves at the far end of the cove. The caves led to another cove, only reachable at low tide. Leaving their things they headed for the dark shadows of the cliffs. Karl, Cass and Ewan laughed and joked about smugglers and wreckers. To them smuggling and wrecking were the stuff of myths and legends – but it wasn't like that for Joel. He'd heard tales of beaches with boats lured in during storms. He knew about contraband. The tea they drank, and the brandy – no-one questioned where they came from, but they all knew. In his day there was nothing to compare with this innocent pleasure on beaches, nor the wonder and awe, the power and beauty of cliffs, the artistry of the sea-hewn rocks.

They made it through to the hidden cove.

It was spread with white untrodden sand, stained with shadows of steep cliffs, where gulls wheeled and dived. Then, for an hour, they explored – pools, caves and rocks – they splashed in the sea... and Joel Penberthy was no longer of his own time. He was, with his three friends, a citizen of the twenty-first century. His belly was full. His limbs bore the healthy weariness of swimming and surfing, while his soul embraced a world that was more wondrous than anything he'd ever known.

Chapter 20

But as they collected their things and made their way to the bus stop, he knew, soon, he'd be stripped of his place here. He'd be pushed into the role of an interloper again. After that he'd be back in his own time.

He didn't say anything on the bus. Suddenly he felt numb. In his own world he faced the threat of the mob, with the Pellar and Hab stirring trouble. It wouldn't be so easy to reach the cottage either, even if he followed the coast road. People down the mine had seen him disappear through a solid wall. Everyone would be in their homes or in ale houses and dram shops, blackening his name. There may even be men watching for him.

He stared through the bus window. At Tehidy he followed the others up the hill, feeling lost and alone.

"You've gone a bit quiet," Cass said. "Didn't you enjoy it on the beach?"

He wanted to cry.

"I enjoyed it more than what I should," he said. "But I ain't going to go on doing that am I? Because, now, I got to be back in the smock and britches. Then I'll be in my own time with nothing to remember but this wondrous dream."

"The portal can bring you here again tomorrow," Ewan said. His smile melted his bronzed face, while his blue eyes softened. "It's worse for me. It's my last day tomorrow. I go back to London, Saturday, and I haven't got any portal to bring me here."

"If I do find the stope tomorrow, a part of me want to come back," Joel said. "But sometimes I wish I could stay for ever."

Ewan looked at Karl. “He could, couldn’t he? With my dad at the foreign office. We could fix something.”

“Yeah, sure,” said Karl. “I mean, my dad bent a few rules to put his father right. What’s to stop your dad bending rules too?”

“Then he’s got to stay,” Cass said.

“But Father and Mother,” Joel said. “I got Father to tend.”

“After that though? When he’s totally OK again,” Cass persisted.

He sighed. “I can’t think proper, beyond Father.”

They were quiet for the rest of the way, but while Joel changed, he could hear them talking. Their voices were low, although they were smiling when he came out of the caravan. “We’re going to do stuff,” Ewan said. “Don’t upset yourself, mate.”

“I ain’t upset,” he said “– not when I be here with you, but… it don’t seem real. It’s Father what’s real.” Thinking of his father, he added, “I got to see the doctor, too, before I go, and Cass’s father. I got a feeling about the mine.”

“We can walk up to the surgery,” Karl said. “I’ll get Dad to drive us over to Cass’s place when we’ve seen him.”

Karl’s father was pleased with what Joel told him about the treatment. But then he went to a shelf and picked out more stuff. It surprised Joel. He thought he’d done everything to cure Father, but the doctor sat at his desk and said, “We’re going to ditch the splints, old lad. Hopefully the broken bone is still in place, but splints won’t do the job. We have to set your father’s leg in plaster.”

He gave Joel a white sock and a new set of instructions. There was fluffy material in a roll to bind the leg, then a third thing, like the cloth he’d used for his father's wound, but this time, the doctor said, he had to soak it in water. Then, straight away, he must bind it over the fluffy material, keeping his father's toes free.

He smiled. "Got all that?" There were other things, so he could get to the wound. It was beginning to sound complicated again. The wet cloth, Dr Greaves said, would set rock hard. It would hold the leg while the bones mended. He also suggested Joel make a crutch so his father could move around.

That would mean another trip to the wood yard. He knew, this time, others would be there. Some of the miners made night-time raids to get wood for their fires – but the whole place was stiff with danger. One more hazard wouldn't make any difference. He loaded the sock and the materials into his croust bag, along with a small scissors, but lying in the bag was his pasty.

"My mother gived me this," he said. "I didn't eat it. We had this handsome fish food down the beach."

Karl turned the pasty over, examining it. "Cass's dad could do something with this," he said. "I mean, it's like – it's genuine eighteenth century, yeah? Like – the prototype of all pasties."

When they got to Cass's house, Mr Blake examined the pasty. He laughed. "So you lot are telling me this is over two hundred years old. Trouble is, you've almost got me believing it – well – accepting it might be more to the point. I mean, you talk the talk, Joel, and you walk the walk. You know just what you ought to for an eighteenth-century guy. You wear the right clothes." He came across, touching the edge of Joel's smock again. "The material's right, and I checked out Wheal Gwenvor. What you said about an apprentice holding the jumping bar is spot on. I know it isn't possible, your story, but... you put up a convincing case." He turned the pasty over and grinned. "So, what with that, and what Phil, here, told me, I reckon I've got to accept that..." He shook his head. "And I need to be certified, saying this, but I suppose I've got to concede this here pasty might be two hundred years old. We'd best freeze it. Later we'll find a way to dry it. Then we can put it in the exhibition down the third level."

But the third level – that was why Joel was there. "Can I see that level again, sir?" he said.

Cass's mother glanced at the clock. "It's a bit late now, Joel," she said. "Could you come over tomorrow? You could spend as long as you liked down there then."

"Can all four of us go?" asked Cass.

"I don't see why not," said Mr Blake. "But Ewan's family will have plans, surely? It's your last day, isn't that right, Ewan?"

Ewan laughed. "My lot will be packing. Dad likes to get away early – beat the Saturday rush. We'll be off some crazy hour, Saturday morning. Going down the mine would be really good. I hate packing."

"Four guests for tomorrow then. It'll be a trial run for Monday."

"What about Monday?" Ewan asked.

Cass climbed onto one of the kitchen stools. "Dad's big opening – Monday night. The mayor's coming – and the Press. We've got the television. They're going to get the steam engine running."

Hearing that alarmed Joel. He didn't know yet what would trigger any disaster, but the idea of the engine and the pumps working on Monday – that wasn't good, and now he knew – he had to be back tomorrow. He had to get down to that third level. "I know it be late, sir," he said, "but – could us take a look at that engine. The one we got come from Mr Watt's foundry, up country..." He tailed off. He didn't want to say too much, not until he was certain.

"That would be awesome," Ewan said.

Cass laughed as Mr Blake stood up. "No worries, Joel. Dad will show you, whatever – whether you want to see it or not."

But the engine Mr Blake showed them was nothing like the beam engine that drove the pumps in Joel's time. It was smaller, more compact. There were a lot more bits to it – wheels and driving pistons. At first Joel thought that might be good. The engine wasn't huge like his beam engine. It wouldn't have the same power – but he was wrong.

"She's a greedy little piece," Mr Blake said. "She uses three times more coal than the old beam engine." He sounded proud. "But she does a heck of a lot more work. She's loads more powerful."

Karl and Ewan were wandering around, examining the structure of shining metalwork, while Joel's mind raced. "If it got that much power," he said. "When it do steam up, Monday, with they things down the mine, the pumps and the man engine, won't it make the ground shift?"

Karl laughed. "It won't start an earthquake, Joel. It isn't that powerful."

But Mr Blake nodded. "It could. Just around the pumps and the man-engine, until they're bedded in, but we've got supports. The ground's pretty stable."

"It's not like your dad's gunpowder disaster," Ewan said.

"But I'm thinking," said Joel. He was staying cautious. "We had this disaster down our mine last week. The old third level got flooded. The pump what we got couldn't clear it. They had to seal it up. They'm digging the new level now. Thing is, I can't work out how close the old and new levels do run. If that engine shift the ground and the levels be too close… I got to look up maps back home, see where the old level do run, because I got this feeling – as if something's going to go wrong when that engine do steam up, Monday."

"I can't see how anything could happen," Mr Blake said. "To my knowledge the new third level has been there for over two hundred years. It hasn't caved in yet. But these maps –"

"I believe they'm in the cap'm's office, sir. I got to get to them, and it got to be at night when all they others is gone home."

Ewan's eyes widened. "What? Break in, you mean?"

"There ain't no other way," he said. "Cap'm Bolitho won't let me look at maps. I couldn't give him no reasons why I want to see them."

"Industrial espionage. That's well cool," Karl said.

"It's so dangerous though. If you got caught," said Cass.

"I got to take that chance," he said. "I got to know where the old level do run."

They were making their way back towards the house. "I wouldn't want you to do anything illegal, son," said Mr Blake.

Joel's mind was set though. "I got to do it, sir – even take one of the maps, so you can see it. Else, how is we going to know if they levels do run too close?"

"There's no way you're going to ask the boy to commit burglary, Alistair," said Mrs Blake.

"I will do it, ma'am. I got to make certain there ain't no disaster, not if you'm opening the mine, Monday."

"I don't see there's a lot I can do if you've set your mind on it," Mr Blake said. He sighed. "But take care, son, and you don't have to purloin any maps. Say I give you a torch. Do you know what that is?"

"Me and the doctor had torches in the stope," he said.

"You can have a camera too. It's a sort of gadget – you take pictures with it – if you took photos of the maps, that would save lifting them. All you do is aim the camera, then capture the pictures. It'll only take seconds. That way you can get clear before anybody catches you. I'll get you familiar with a camera when we're in the house."

They went through to the kitchen, while Mr Blake fetched the torch. He also brought something that looked like a small black box which, he explained, was the camera. The first thing Joel did was take a photo of Cass, then one of her with Karl and Ewan. When he looked, the pictures were as clear as the likeness Cass had left for him in the bottle. It excited him. He could carry images of his friends into his own world – and look at them just at the touch of a button.

Mr Blake explained how, when he'd found the plans, he had to shine the torch and try to get all the plan into the picture. He suggested taking up to ten photos, just in case some didn't come out clearly.

"It's more like industrial espionage every minute," Ewan said.

But, with the torch and camera, Joel had a truer idea of what he was going to do. He put them in his croust bag along with the medical packages from Dr Greaves.

Then… it was time. He had to go back.

He didn't say much in the car going to Tehidy, nor as they climbed the hill.

At the edge of the stope, Karl and Ewan gave him the usual hugs. He was getting used to that, but Cass's eyes seemed deep, as though she understood the things that were raging in his head. She kissed him like she had when they'd said goodbye the previous day. "Be safe," she whispered. "We'll wait for you up here tomorrow, the same time. And I'll be scared out of my head until I see you."

"Yeah, with the espionage and stuff we all will," said Karl. "Specially with those crap idiots trying to do you in."

Chapter 21

There was a weight of fumes when he got back. His pupils strained, searching for a hint of light. All around were sounds; scuttering rats, the tired groans of wooden props. Every now and again stones splashed into a sett as the mine fell back into repose.

He groped his way, with sharp pieces of rock poking his flesh. His back knocked against supporting props, until he sensed the shaft close by. He had to be careful feeling for the ladder. One false step and he'd be falling to his death, but once he'd managed to put a foot on the first rung it was easier. He clung on, groping up the shaft, afraid of what might be waiting for him at the pithead.

When he got there, though, there was nothing, except for the torches in the wood yard – the shadows of men foraging. With the clouds heavy and no moon or starlight, he was able to search out the timber he needed for his father's crutch. But he didn't know what kind of welcome he'd get when he reached home. If Rose was there, or Hab, or the Pellar, his parents would know he'd been down the mine.

Pushing open the cottage door, he propped the wood against the wall. His mother was at the table, kneading pastry. But the Pellar was there, crouched by the fire. Rose was by the fire too. Obadiah sat cross legged on the floor. His father was asleep.

"Where's Hab?" he said.

"He'm out looking for you, with Sam Eustice," said his mother. She leaned her hands on the table and added: "There been some strange tales about you today, boy. And to tell the truth, I can't make much sense of them. They'm saying you was down the pit. You never told us you was going down no pit. They'm telling you disappeared through a solid wall, and that don't fit with nothing I can get hold of."

"Who have Hab got out there with him, other than Sam Eustice?" he said.

She began pummelling the dough again. "There be a few. But what I want to know is, how was it you was down that mine? And what's this about going through solid rock?"

There wasn't much he could say, especially with the Pellar there, and it was best to leave it until his mother had calmed down. Besides, his head was wrestling with what he must do for Father.

"I been to see the doctor," he said. "He gived me new treatments. I got to do something with Father's leg, and he do need his potion again."

"Is you letting that boy near your husband with they poisons, woman?" the Pellar demanded.

Joel watched his mother turn from the Pellar to his father. "Them things don't sit right with me," she said.

But now Father was awake. He'd pulled himself up on the pallet. "Like I told you, Mother, it be his potions what have saved me. You leave him be."

Joel knelt beside him and said, "I got to take that splint away, Father. I got to put something else on your leg, what will hold firm while the bone do mend."

Carefully he removed the dressing and the two supporting pieces of wood. After that he called Obadiah and Rose. Rose was reluctant, but his mother gave her a brief nod and she came across. He was anxious though, afraid moving the splint might have dislodged the bone. As quickly as he could he slid the doctor's sock onto the foot. It seemed to stretch, fitting easily; but the Pellar leapt up when he took the scissors to cut a hole by the toes.

"See how they things do sparkle," she hissed. "Twinkly pieces from hell. They been forged in Satan's fires."

His mother was looking – questioning. "They don't look right," she said. "Shining like that." But he didn't answer. He was struggling to remember every word of the doctor's instructions.

He bound the leg with the fluffy material, then unrolled the binding cloth. He knew the next step had to be quick. Taking a bucket from by the fire, he plunged the cloth into water, wringing it out. Then he bound it onto the leg, cutting a hole so he could get to the wound; but soon after he'd finished, the door flung open and Hab stood there. "The runt's back then," he snorted. "And what's he doing now?"

He barged across, poking at the leg.

The bandage was already drying. "That be more of his devilry," he growled. He stood away, swearing. "There be heat coming from that."

Joel touched the cloth. It *was* warm. Now though, the Pellar was stumbling towards it. She put her hand on it and what, moments ago, had been a supple cloth, soaked in cold water, had changed to a firm, warm casement.

"Can't you see it, woman?" she hissed, glaring at Joel's mother. "That boy be possessed. Tonight we seen it with our own eyes – the devil at work in this house. That thing was nothing but cloth a minute ago. Now it be turned like a hot shell."

"He be worse than a snivelling warlock," Hab rasped. "He ain't fit to live." He was steering Rose to the door. Then he turned. "I'm coming back, Mother. Don't you fret, and you got to give up on that brat. You seen what devilry he'm doing."

He seized the Pellar's pot, storming out, with the old woman and Rose following.

"It ain't right, Mother – What Hab do say. It ain't true," Joel said.

"But that thing on your father's leg," said his mother. "It be doing things what isn't natural. That wasn't no more than a bit of wet cloth a minute ago. Look at it now, hard as a shell – and giving off heat, Hab do say."

"It don't feel like nothing of the devil to me," his father said. "It do feel comfortable enough."

Joel touched the surface of the cast again. It was already losing heat, but now it was as hard as stone. He fetched the two pieces of wood from by the door, while his mother moved from the table. She settled, facing the fire, staring at the flames.

"Fetch me nails and the mallet, Obadiah," he said. "The doctor said I got to make a crutch for Father. If he have that to lean on, he can move about."

"Who exactly is this doctor?" demanded his mother. She was tight-lipped. "The Pellar do say he'm some kind of villain born out of hell."

This, though, was too much for his father. "In the Lord's name, woman, you'm swinging around like a sail in the wind. One minute you'm out fighting for the boy against a rabble of drunks, the next minute you'm siding with them."

"But it be hard, Amos," she said. "What he'm doing – them little things he do give you, it ain't natural. Anyone can see that."

Joel began to work on the crutch, resting the longer piece of wood between his legs, nailing the shorter piece to the top.

"Look, Mother," he said at last, "I told Mr Jewell – and Rose – there be something strange going on. But what's happening be harder to get hold of than you thinking I'm working with Satan."

He saw his mother's face tighten. "In the Lord's name, Joel, boy," she hissed. "What you been doing that be more impossible than siding with the devil?"

He began to bind the cloth from the splint to the top of the crutch, making a cushion for his father's arm; but he knew this couldn't go on. At last he said, "Mother, Father, I'm going to tell you what I never thought I'd ever tell. I got to tell it though, so you know it ain't no devil what's looking after Father."

"Dear Jesus," his mother whispered. She was still sitting with her hands clasped, staring into the fire. But his father was alive with curiosity.

"Go on then, boy," he said.

"Well," said Joel. "It started when I come back late from croust that day."

His father was watching, listening to every word. Obadiah's mouth was open. "It be true," he said. "I went up a stope today. But they men what was chasing me, they was right too. To them it looked like I went through solid rock. It's only me what can find the stope. It's only me what can go into it."

"Then it be the devil's work, boy," his mother said.

"It ain't, Mother. It be something bigger than that."

He took a deep breath, plunging into his story, but he could see his mother, shutting her mind. At one point she poked the fire. Her face was strained. "It ain't right," she said, putting her hand up. "I don't want to hear no more."

But his father insisted. "Yes you do, woman. You'm keen enough to listen to Habakkuk and the Pellar when they spew up their poison. You let the boy speak."

Joel could hardly believe what he was doing, but he knew this was the only way. He told them about Cass, the boys, Dr Greaves, the amazing inventions of their world.

Every now and again his mother interrupted. “No, boy. I don’t want to hear.” She was looking away, refusing to catch his eye. At last she stood up. “It be fanciful nonsense. Something what you dreamed up.”

“The cures, though, Mother,” he persisted. “They things what I brought back to help Father, they ain’t fanciful.”

She shook her head, sitting down again. “My mind is full of confusion. I don’t know what to believe no more.”

“There be other things what will prove it,” he said. He’d finished building the crutch. Now he reached for his croust bag. “These be things what they gived me – things I might need back here, and they ain’t magic. They ain’t no more magic than our beam engine.”

He held up the torch, while Obadiah stared. “They can harness a power what do make lightning,” he said. “It be called electricity. They put it in this torch, look.” He switched on the torch, while his mother threw her hands to her eyes.

“The Good Lord preserve us,” she gasped.

Then he took the camera. “Take a look at this, Mother, and you Obadiah. They made this little box what do capture likenesses. This afternoon I took a likeness of Cass, then another of all of them, all three, Cass, Karl and Ewan.”

He searched for the images, and his mother squinted at the picture of Cass. “You’m telling me that’s a maid,” she said. “She don’t look like no maid to me. She got short hair, and she be wearing boy’s britches. That ain’t fitty, not how no maid should be going on.”

"It's what they wear, Mother. Look – all three of them. They'm kind people, warm and good. That be Karl, and that one, he'm Ewan, and look, Cass again."

She was shaking her head. "They don't look right. They ain't wearing fitty clothes, and – how do that thing work? Some person painting a likeness like that would take days."

"Here, Father, you look," he said. "I could take an image of you. You come over here Mother, and Obadiah – stand by Father."

His mother was reluctant, but finally she came over.

The image on the camera's screen was dull, but when he pressed the 'take' button, a flash blistered through the room that made his mother cry out in terror. "What in the name of evil was that?" she said. "Lightning, flashing in this room, and dear God, my sight been took away."

Joel was as surprised as she was. He hadn't expected the camera to do that, but, when he looked, the image was bright and clear, his mother and father, and Obadiah.

Mother was back by the fire now, sitting down, shaking. At last she muttered, "Thank Jesus our Saviour. My vision may be coming back."

But Joel had his image. "See, Father," he said, "and you, Obadiah, you'm there, with Mother, just like you was a minute ago."

"That be wonderful, boy," his father said. "And these people, they do make all these things?"

"They done more than that," he said. "They made things what light up a room if you touch something in the wall, doors what can open on their own when they see you coming. They got carts that don't need no horses, what can get from here to London in six hours, and they made they potions what brought you back from death, Father – they made all them things."

His mother clicked her fingers. “Here, boy. I may as well see what nonsense this box have done, now the good Lord have given me back my sight.”

He showed her the picture; but she shook her head. “It ain’t no good. I can’t accept it. I can’t believe it happened.”

“Well, I can,” his father said. “I believe it all. The boy have been into future years, and he’ve found people what have brought me back from death’s door, and that, Mother, do make them good people. Like Joel said; they’m good hearted. You only got to look at the image of them three, two handsome boys and a maid with a kind face, no matter if she do look like a boy.”

His mother still didn’t move. “It would be a miracle if it were true,” she said.

“You still ain’t believing me, are you, Mother?” said Joel.

“I can’t deny it be hard,” she said. “But what do worry me is Habakkuk. He’m already fanning the fire. If he ever see they things, or hear what you just said, he’ll be worse by more miles than you could run. He’m coming back, too. By my thinking, you’d best be well clear of here when he come. You don’t want to be around to face that mob again.”

“I ain’t going,” Joel said. “– Not tonight. I ain’t running off to hide like some child. My place be here, to protect you.”

“If you stay,” his father said, “and that lot have their way, you ain’t going to be nowhere to protect no-one. There ain’t no shame in leaving it to your mother, boy. There ain’t a man in this region what got the stomach to stand up to she. It be well known. You get over to Billy Jewell’s.”

His mother's face didn't flinch. "You go on, son. I got no fear of Habakkuk or his band of idiots."

"Father's little pellet, though," he said. "He got to have another one before bed."

"You can leave they with me. I can see they isn't doing him no harm. I'll give him the pellet tonight, and don't you take no risks, coming over tomorrow. I can give him another three then. You stay low, out the way."

She'd already put his croust bag over his shoulder, steering him towards the door. But, as he stumbled into the night, he felt the shame again. He was a coward, a child hiding under the protection of his mother. Worse, he was afraid Hab and his band of drunks might not succumb to her tongue so easily tonight.

Chapter 22

Billy had heard about him passing through a wall. He seemed unsettled. "I see how people do think it be dark practices, boy. I would too if I didn't know you better."

"It's a mess, though," said Mary. "Billy told me you ain't safe no more, not with that crowd hounding you."

But now, what Billy and Mary were doing presented him with a dilemma. "If they find out you'm hiding me..." he said, "That don't seem right. I shouldn't be staying here."

"You'll leave over my dead body," said Billy. "You'm a good boy – It be my Christian duty… I had a word with the underground cap'm today. He got a mind to go up and see Father, Saturday. I'd like to go too, if that be all right. I ain't seen Amos since the level comed down."

The mention of the underground captain, though, brought reality to Joel's night time plans. At some time he had to get to the captain's office. He still didn't know how he was going to do it. He'd have to go from the cottage – and there seemed no good time for that. The office was in the centre of Redruth. If one of the family woke while he was away – or if he was seen in Redruth... He knew of the building where the offices were. It was a huge rambling place, and – even if he could find a way in, he had no idea where the captain's office was, or if the plans were there. They existed, he was certain of that. He'd seen the captain with some of the mine owners and venturers, studying them. There were so many hazards though.

But later he seized his time, when the cottage was heavy with sleep.

There was no break in the clouds, and the darkness across the moors was opaque. From Billy Jewell's the journey into Redruth was shorter, although there were perils – hidden hedges, gaping lesions in the earth, sleeping cattle – and the threat from cottage doors and dram shops, where the hangouts of a night's drinking might be lying in their drunken stupor.

Redruth was quiet, but even the deserted streets posed a challenge. If the night-watchman caught him, there would be no escape.

When he reached the mine office, what in his memory had been a fortress looming and unattainable, now seemed utterly impenetrable.

Without any plan, he groped along the walls, searching out the small passage he knew lay between this building and the next. If he could get around the back he could use his torch, but every move shivered on his flesh.

At last, though, he found the end of the wall and began to feel his way down the narrow passage. But that was as far as he got. As he edged, moving his feet in a cautious sideways motion, there was an obstruction. His body was unstable and he stumbled.

Immediately the obstruction uncurled itself, letting out a slurred yell of, "Hell's teeth."

Joel could feel his foot being grabbed. Desperately he struggled to regain his balance, pulling himself free, while his assailant fought in an ale-induced stupor.

Now the drunk was bawling, "Help! It be cut-throats. They got my purse. I been robbed." Scrambling to his feet, he made another grab for Joel.

But Joel had the advantage of a clear head. Frantically he slid between the wall and the lumbering man, staggering back onto the street. The drunk was still stumbling after him, yelling, making enough noise to rouse the dead.

Already Joel knew his plan to get into the mine office was in tatters; but, worse, now he could make out the light of a lantern further down the road. For one moment he froze as he heard the night-watchman's voice calling him to a halt.

Then, with his fleetness of foot, taking advantage of the darkness and confusion, he ran – out past streets, past dram shops and ale houses, into the blackness of fields and hedgerows, struggling with his instinct and memory to find his way back to Billy Jewell's cottage.

For a while, he grasped the cottage wall, fighting for breath, shaking with shock and exhaustion.

For the second time in one day, he'd been one hair's breadth away from capture.

Eventually he eased the door open.

To his relief the cottage room was silent – with nothing more than the regular breathing of heavy sleep. He crept back to his place, although his head was in turmoil.

He still hadn't seen the map. There was nothing to help save Mr Blake's mine. His only hope was, he might find something when Cass's father took him down to the level later that day, something that clearly wasn't right.

He could hardly get himself off the floor in the morning. Mrs Jewell gave him a dish of tea and a piece of bread before leaving, but he didn't dare look through the window until there was clear daylight. Only when he was sure everyone had gone to the pit did he make his move.

Although his mother had told him not to come back, the first thing he did was cross to his parents' cottage, afraid of what Hab and his mob might have done. But the small, white building with its sagging stone roof – the wisp of smoke that drifted from the chimney – it was all there. He didn't go in. He only needed to know his family was safe.

Now he had other things on his mind.

He couldn't shake off the memory of yesterday, the chase in the mine – or that encounter with the drunk. He was frantic to slide into the future without having to go down the pit. His thoughts searched for some different route to the portal… Perhaps the exit to the stope behind Tehidy. If that stope was there in his own time, the portal might take him into the twenty-first century on a reverse path. He would pass through time as he climbed down, so he would come out in Mr Blake's mine. It would mean he'd never have to go down the pit to get to Cass's world again.

He made his way towards Tehidy's woods, pulling his clothes around him against the wind.

The contours of the moors had only changed slightly. He could recognise the hill with its winter-bitten gorse and scrub. He was certain this was where the stope came out; where he met Cass and the boys, but, when he climbed, he could find nothing – just wild grassland, with a few rocks and boulders.

He'd set his heart on discovering a different route, and now he felt desperate. He'd have to try Carn Brae. If he could find a route down the shaft where Mr Blake's office was... But, again, there was nothing except windblown moorlands and scrub. At last the realisation gripped him. The only way into the stope was back in the mine, with its shafts and levels. He'd have to dodge men who might be lying in wait for him. He'd already endured two chases. Now he was terrified he wouldn't be able to slip to the second level without being discovered.

His eyes were darting everywhere as he changed into his smock. But he knew the mine would cloak him. Sometimes the miners put their candles out to save the air. The tributors often did. They had to buy their own candles. It made them very careful about using them. If by some miracle no-one saw him, he would search out the stope at croust time.

As he clambered towards the level though, everything felt sour – the stifling heat, the noise, the rumble of trucks, the sharp rhythms of hammers and pick-axes. Today the sounds numbed his brain. In the twilight of struggling candles, his imagination saw eyes – in the floor, in the walls. There was a sweat on him, making his body shake. He kept close to the rock-face, sliding from shadow to shadow. When a boy came by, he pressed against the wall, holding his breath, searching out the darkest recess.

He didn't know how he was going to stay hidden. With each step, his breathing became more shallow, confusing his mind. One false move, and he knew that would be the end for him.

Further down the level there was a truck not being used. He decided it would be safer to hide in that. But every time someone came near, or he heard the rumble of another truck, his breathing stopped. There was a moment when he thought he would pass out.

At last, though, he heard the tramp of men and boys, with calls from those coming up from the third level. He didn't move until he was sure they'd all gathered for their croust. Then, with as much caution as he could muster, he eased himself back into the mine.

His head swam as he staggered along the face of rock, but finally the ground started to rise. He was groping among strewn boulders again. The air was cooler. The tang of salt touched his nostrils, although, today, he wasn't sure. He still had no idea about saving Mr Blake's mine, and he had no plans for what he'd do in the third level.

Chapter 23

It was Karl who greeted him, gripping his hand, putting an arm around his shoulder. “We were dead worried, mate,” he said.

Cass looked pale. “It kept me awake all night.”

“It were a bit of a scare back there,” he admitted. “My brother, Hab, I think he put men in the pit, watching out for me. I had to hide in a cart till croust time. I haven’t got no pictures of the maps yet, neither. I got tangled with a drunk when I went to the mine office.”

“I wish you’d stay here,” said Cass. “Ewan’s dad would fix it.”

They were walking towards Polgwenvor.

But when they reached the main road, Cass took a silver object from her pocket, putting it to her ear. She seemed to think it was her father because she was calling it ‘Dad’, telling it that Joel was here and they were on their way.

Karl laughed. “It’s her phone,” he said, and Cass grinned.

“Here, Dad. Say ‘Hi’ to Joel. He thinks I’m talking to myself.”

She put the silver thing to his ear and... he could hear Mr Blake’s voice. It said, “How you doing then, Joel?”

His eyes were darting around in amazement. “Where’s he to?” he gasped. “I do hear him, but I don’t see nothing.”

The voice came again. “We’re over Burger King. We thought we’d get some food inside us before we went down the mine.”

“He said he’m over Burger King,” he whispered. “But I can’t see no Burger King, yet I do hear his voice, talking.”

“We can talk to people all over the world with these. Everybody’s got one,” Ewan said.

Now Cass was telling the thing to get Joel a bacon double cheeseburger with fries. She spoke to it some more, then put it back in her britches pocket, and however unbelievable, when they got to Burger King, Mr and Mrs Blake were there, and Mr Blake knew. He’d ordered the food, including Joel’s bacon double cheeseburger with fries.

After they’d eaten, they drove to the mine, where, on their descent, they stopped at the man-engine. Ewan said, “That looks well dangerous. Say they missed their footing?” He wanted to know if that was how Joel went down the mine.

“We don’t have no such thing,” Joel told him. “We do climb down on wood ladders.”

But the sight of the man-engine made him shudder. On Monday, when that contraption and the pumps woke up, something bad was going to happen.

He could sense it even more when they reached the third level – the silence and heat, the breathless glow of the lozenged lights. He stared at the men and boys in their miner’s clothes, at the unreal sight of motionless trucks and stacked kibbles. A boy with a waxy face was holding a loaded kibble nearby, not moving. It was as if the whole place hung… waiting.

Karl’s and Ewan’s eyes were darting everywhere.

“They’ve got smocks like yours,” Karl said. “This is real cool, Alistair.”

“Is that like the cart you hid in before you found the stope?” Cass asked.

Mr Blake looked questioningly.

"He had to hide," Cass told him. "He's on the run. They think he's messing with the devil – the way he's curing his dad."

"Really, Joel?" said Mrs Blake. "That can't be right, surely?"

"It be true, ma'am," he said. "But I got my parents and the underground cap'm. There be Billy Jewell, too. They do make sure I won't come to no harm."

They walked along the level, and all the time he was looking for signs.

"It's seriously hot down here," Ewan said.

"Yeah, why's that?" Karl asked.

"We're in the bowels of the earth aren't we?" said Mr Blake. "You've heard of hot rocks, yes – heated by the Earth's magma? Well, around here those rocks come near the surface. The deeper we go, the nearer we get to them – so – the hotter the levels get."

By now Joel could sense they were approaching the shaft that he used, but when they reached it, there was a wall, with a metal door. "We had to shut it off," Mr Blake explained. "Health and safety. But I've had new ladders put in. It'll serve as our emergency exit through that door."

Somehow he felt reassured that the shaft was still there, but, always, running at the back of his mind were thoughts of floods and floating wax bodies. There was one place in particular that was drawing him. He'd had an uneasy feeling about it the last time they were there – the way it dipped, beyond the lift.

"That don't look right," he said.

"They were probably following the line of a lode," Mr Blake explained. "Or there could have been a bit of granite, too hard to blast out."

But when they went down the passage into the dip, Joel stopped. A deep cut had been excavated – with artefacts laid out on one side – and on the other, a sparsely furnished room something like his own cottage. A sign said: '*The interior of a typical miner's dwelling in the eighteenth century*'.

"That's the work of my engineers," said Mr Blake. "It'll be the centre-piece of the exhibition. We animated the people in the room so they move and talk." He looked at Karl and Ewan. "That'll draw the punters in, don't you reckon?"

"When we come back in the summer, I'll bring Mum and Dad down here," Ewan said.

But, for Joel, this cut was wrong, although, as the afternoon headed towards evening, he still wasn't clear how it was wrong. He hadn't learned all he'd hoped to. In the lift back to grass he said, "Have you got maps what show how the mine do run in these times, sir? If you got them, I could make an image on the camera. Then I could see how close the two third levels run."

"You don't need a camera," Mr Blake said, smiling. "I can copy maps for you, then you can have a map of your own. But, to be honest, I still can't see where there's any danger."

They crossed to the office where he took a sheet of paper from a drawer, putting it into a machine. Joel watched the machine swallow the paper, before spitting it out again. But there was another sheet which Mr Blake handed to him. "Your own copy," he said, patting the machine. "This thing's like a camera. It takes photos of papers and documents."

"And I can keep what you gived me?" Joel asked.

"It's yours to do what you like with."

Mrs Blake smiled. "Do you need to go yet, Joel?"

“I daren’t, ma’am,” he said “– not till they be finished with the shift and there ain’t no people down the mine. But it don’t make no difference. I can wait up by Tehidy.”

“No,” she said. “We were hoping you wouldn’t have to go. Cass wants us to do a barbecue. What about you, Ewan, or do your parents need you?”

“I could call them,” said Ewan.

When they reached the house they went into the garden. Joel had seen the garden before, through the window, but being outside made it so different. The grass was cut to the level of carpet pile. There were flower beds blazing with yellows, whites, reds and blues – and a pool, set in a scree of rocks. When Mr Blake went into the house he must have done something, because water started tumbling over the rocks.

There was a large slab area laid out, with a stone structure built on it. Cass and Mrs Blake moved a table towards the structure. Then they brought out bread and other food. When Mr Blake touched a button, the stone thing burst into flames. After that he went into the house again; coming out wearing a green apron, carrying metal objects, as if he was planning to do the cooking. No man Joel knew could ever do cooking.

He was consumed by the novelty, while the smells wafting from the stone structure tantalized him.

“Is this how you do cook your food?” he asked.

“Only on warm evenings, usually in high summer,” Mrs Blake said. “Any time Alastair wants to show off his culinary skills. Normally we cook in the kitchen. In there he’s got as much skill as an orang-utan making a soufflé.”

“It’s all in your honour,” laughed Mr Blake. “And the fact that this warm spell is going to break tomorrow. The forecast is for squally showers and longer spells of rain.”

Joel stared. “You do know what the weather be doing tomorrow? And you said ‘rain’. All the time I been here, except for that first day, the sun been shining. I was thinking, with all they inventions, you could make it shine all the time.”

“I wish,” said Ewan.

They fetched food off the stove – beefburgers, like the ones in Burger King; then there were amazingly flavoured wings from chickens, and strange vegetables mixed with pieces of meat on sticks. Like all the food, it had flavours that were so amazing, better than anything he’d ever tasted.

When Mr Blake finished cooking, he put the remainder of the food on a shelf above the stove, and settled in one of the chairs. “So, Joel,” he said. “Cass tells me you couldn’t get photos of the maps. It sounds like that office place is pretty well secure.”

“I got to get them, sir,” he said. “And when I seen them, I got to come back, Monday.”

“Don’t do it, son,” said Mr Blake. “It’s too risky. We’ve trialled the steam engine. Nothing’s going to happen. It’ll be safe enough.”

But, for Joel, the signs were there. “I got to do it – so I’m sure. It be all right. I ain’t going to get caught.”

Later though, when they arrived at the portal’s entrance, he was feeling less confident. The goodbyes seemed to herald a moment of dread – and there was a sadness.

Ewan held him for a long time. “It’s been awesome, Joel, mate – meeting you,” he said. “It’s been the best thing that’s ever happened to me, and… you’ve got to be here when we come down again in the Summer, right?”

He didn’t feel embarrassed. What Ewan said gave him a warmth that was hard to put into words. He was feeling a deep love for this handsome, fair-haired boy, and for Karl and Cass. He couldn't accept that the centuries would ever separate them.

Karl wasn't so expressive. He just said, "Good luck, mate, you know – with all that crap – the espionage and stuff. Make sure you don't get caught."

Cass, though, was near crying. "It won't be the same," she whispered. "You coming out of that stope each day. What will you do Monday, when me and Karl are back at school?"

"I won't have no trouble," he said. "I been here enough times to know the way."

"Couldn't you come tomorrow, or Sunday?" she pleaded. "It isn't till Monday we go back to school."

But he shook his head. "I got to find they plans. It'll be hard making a time – when it be safe."

Then he moved towards the stope. As he went, though, he tried to burn an indelible image of his three friends into his memory. He wanted to picture them for ever, just as they were at that moment – especially Ewan. It may be he would never see Ewan again – and that was something he could hardly bear contemplate.

Chapter 24

Because it was late, he went straight to Billy Jewell's. He trusted his mother to give Father the three pellets. But Billy greeted him with news that threw him: "I had another word with the underground cap'm today, boy," he said. "He want me to bring you across to his place tomorrow, before he go up to see Father."

"He'm thinking to take you under his wing, Joel, boy," said Mary. "– See no harm do come to you. He said you'll be staying at his place from now on. Your brother won't come near you, not when you'm up with the cap'm."

But staying with the captain, he knew, would make everything so much more difficult – and to break into Captain Bolitho's office when he was living under his roof – that made the furtive deception of what he was planning even worse.

The captain's house was in a street near the centre of town, granite-grey and sturdy, with steps leading to the front door.

When they arrived, next morning, the captain was waiting in his great coat and boots. "I'm keen to see how your father's doing, Joel," he said. "And I got to say, boy, the talk down the mine don't seem kind to you. Gossip – it be like the wind fanning a flame."

His father was still in bed when they reached the cottage. Obadiah had already fetched in water. His mother was working with her lard and flour, making pastry, but when she saw Billy and the captain she dropped the dough, struggling out of her apron. "Cap'm Bolitho," she said. "And Billy Jewell? We wasn't expecting no company. If I'd knowed you was coming, Cap'm, I'd have tidied around a bit."

"Don't fret yourself, Mrs Penberthy," said the captain. "I just came by with the boy here, and Billy, to see how Amos is doing. It be good to see you looking so well, Amos." He looked at the plaster cast, turning to Joel. "Be this some of your handiwork, boy?"

"It do support his leg," Joel explained. "I put the leg straight, but Father need that till the bones knit."

His father had eased himself into a sitting position. "What he've done is nothing short of a miracle, Cap'm. He've made a crutch for me, too. It do help me get about."

"You'll be a cripple when they bones be mended, though," the captain said.

"That ain't what Joel do say. He say, when I get this thing off, my leg will be straight, like new."

He pushed himself up from the bed, hobbling to a chair. Captain Bolitho's eyes followed him and Joel heard him murmur, "The lame man shall leap." Then he added, "I can't say I seen nothing that smacks of black deeds, Amos." He took a seat by the fire. "It look like the boy done wonders. I've had to meet up with the practices of black arts in my time, but what Joel be doing don't bear no resemblance."

"That's just how we do feel, Cap'm," his mother said. "I didn't always see it, but I'm coming round to thinking what he've done is the work of the Almighty."

"He'd be safest biding with me in Redruth for the time being, though – with all the bad feeling down the mine," the captain said. "I'm thinking to take him under my wing. I'll make time for him to come up every day to give you your treatment, Amos. I heard tell he can read and write. I thought we might find him a position in the mine office. Doing that would keep him away from the likes of Habakkuk and Sam Eustice."

"That would be wonderful, Cap'm. My boy, working up the mine office," said his mother. "What do you think, Father?"

"It would be the safest place till all this have blowed over," his father said.

But Joel's head was reeling again. Working in the mine office might make it easier to locate the maps, but... it would cut him off from the mine, and his only access to Cass and her world.

Immediately after they'd visited Father, the captain took him to Redruth, guiding him into the fortress-like building. First they came to a kind of hall. It was huge, with paintings hanging from the walls; likenesses of the Bassets and other mine owners; the gentry from the Pendarves estate; the squire from Godolphin Manor. There were oak tables stretching the length of the hall, laid out with dishes, plates and goblets. Knives, forks and spoons were set on the table. In glass cases by the wall stood huge silver salvers and salt cellars – wealth beyond Joel's imagination.

"This be the Stannary Hall, where the mine owners and adventurers do meet up," the captain said. "They do feast into the small hours here, boy, every quarter, sharing out the takings. You'll serve at tables for the next meeting." He patted Joel on the back, smiling. "They say there be rich pickings in the kitchen for they that serve."

The offices were above the hall. Here he met with men and boys sitting at long desks, their ledgers lit with candles and tapers.

The captain took the chief clerk to one side. "The boy can read and write," he said. "And he be competent with number. I was thinking you might article him to a clerk, see how he take to it. He'm a fast learner." But while they were talking, Joel was scanning the room. He could see plans hanging from the walls, with the names of mines written underneath. There was one he recognised, by the door.

"Would that be Wheal Gwenvor?" he said.

"Can you decipher it, boy?" asked the chief clerk.

It was all there. "That be the shaft," he said. "And look, the stopes and adits. I do see the second level – and that old third level, the one what flooded. I can work out where it go, out under the sea – where the rocks fractured, bringing the water in."

The chief clerk looked at the captain. "He'm bright," he said. He turned to Joel again. "And you don't have no trouble reading and writing? Have you got good penmanship?"

"My reading, sir, that be better than my writing. But I was learned both."

It was agreed that he be freed so he could tend his father, and he spent the rest of the day learning to copy into ledgers. But all the time his brain plotted. That night he had to get back here, with his torch and his camera.

Captain Bolitho had taken him to the kitchen while they'd been down in the Stannary Hall. He'd noticed a window there, with a broken catch. It was small, but – he thought he could squeeze through. He calculated the window was around the back, where he'd been trying to go when he fell against the drunken man.

After visiting his father that evening, he made his way back to Redruth, heading for the Hall. He'd already explained to the underground captain that he might be late, but the prospect of what he was going to do terrified him. It was against every law in the land to break into the mine office. If he got caught, no one would believe he was there to look at the plans of Wheal Gwenvor – not with all that silver in the casements downstairs.

He could hear bawdy laughter and songs from the ale houses and dram shops, but it was a cold night. There weren't too many people about, and by the mine office, the road stood empty.

He crept into the passage and around the back, where he found the broken window. Struggling, he pushed his body through. He was so tight with tension, he could hardly breathe, and he was wrestling with his croust bag, with the camera and torch in it. But then, carefully, he eased himself down, groping his way through the Hall.

By the time he reached the office, though, he was in a sweat. His hands trembled so much as he reached for the torch, he could barely hold it.

But, as he was about to switch it on, he froze.

He could hear a creaking, and steady footsteps on the stairs. For a moment every limb in his body turned to ice.

The footsteps were getting nearer. He could see no way of getting out, and he was certain this office was the room the steps were heading for.

Making a massive effort to free his frozen limbs, he scuttled towards the long desks, sliding underneath, finding the farthest corner, curling into a tight ball. Then he cowered, listening as the door creaked open. A shaft of candlelight shuddered across the floor. Behind it came two dark shadows. One leaned towards the desk, with the man's britches just a few feet from where he was hidden.

There was a drawer being opened at the far end, and a voice, muttering.

Suddenly fear turned to dismay. The voice he was listening to said, "These be they, Matty – the Pendarves accounts, and by the Lord, I was right. Look. Last quarter's return. It was three times what they told us.

They be short-changing us. We got to have it out with them." The voice belonged to Captain Bolitho. If the captain caught him, nothing could save him.

He stared, as one of the two men dragged the candle across the desk. Both captains stood still for a moment, but then, without being able to control his movements, his leg twitched, rocking a stool on the uneven floor. His eyes flashed panic – while the sweat on his body grew cold.

"Be there somebody in here?" he heard the other voice say.

Like a cornered animal, he curled further under the desk, watching the reflective light of the candles. He could see the two men lowering themselves, until the other captain muttered, "Vermin. They be a plague. They do get everywhere."

Then, to his relief, the candle-flame moved back into the room, and he heard the drawer slide shut. At last the spectral shadows began to move out of the room, but he hardly dared let air escape from his lungs. It was like a warning from God. What he was doing was wrong. If the captains had caught him, it would have meant gaol – or even hanging.

For what seemed like an eternity he lay, unable to shift, listening as the footsteps descended the stairs. His thoughts were in turmoil, generating a shame that he couldn't put into words. The captain was sheltering him in his home, yet he was betraying every trust that had been shown to him…

But his mission wasn't wicked. He was doing this for Cass, for Mr Blake – to save people in another world. He'd been given a vision of the future. It was his duty to act. He had to photograph the maps. He had to find out where the danger lay.

It was an age, though, before he managed to shift his legs and crawl from under the desk.

Cautiously he took the camera, struggling to remember Mr Blake's instructions. He knew, to take the photos, he needed the torch. If the two captains were still in the building... Quietly he crept to the door. But he couldn't hear anything. He had to take courage. Closing the door again he switched the torch on. The intensity of light nearly made him drop it. Anyone who happened to be in the street would certainly see. He had to move quickly, too, and it wasn't easy. It took deep breaths to steady himself, but then – ten sharp flashes… and it was done. He glanced at one of the pictures. The image was clear, although he was hating every minute of this.

Now all his instincts were to get away. He hitched his croust bag over his shoulder, making for the kitchen, more scared than he had ever been – afraid that the captains were still in the building, or he'd be found by the night-watchman. It was only a miracle that allowed him to climb back through the window undetected.

Then, dropping into the alleyway, he collapsed into a terrified heap.

The following day, his morning had to be spent tending Father. In the afternoon Captain Bolitho, who was a member of the newly formed Methodist church, wanted him to go with his family to chapel, to listen to a travelling evangelist.

It was only late that evening when he finally found time and space to investigate the course of the old third level. He'd been given a room in the captain's attic. When he managed to escape there, he set to work with the torch and Cass's magic pen. But his tracing of the old level surprised him. It showed the level running some way from the new level – until the dip occurred. Only then did the two levels come close. Yet he still couldn't see any weakness to suggest a flood.

In the morning, at his desk, he tried to picture the old third level, and he could recall it – every twist – where the level bent, where it climbed, and... suddenly he froze.

In the old level there had been a sharp bend following a lode. The twist would be where the new level dipped. There would have been no danger before Mr Blake dug that cut. But the twist in the old level would be running right over the cut and… he knew... it was here the breach would happen.

For the rest of the day he couldn't think about anything else.

He told the chief clerk he needed to leave early to get to his father, but when he'd been released, it was the mine he headed for.

Men, boys and bal maidens were already on their way home. He had to find shelter behind hedges, although by the time he reached the mine the workers had all gone.

Careful to keep himself hidden, he darted around the back of the vanning field. But then he stopped – staring in dismay.

He could see tapers and dark shapes at the shaft's entrance. Sam Eustice was there, and another man. He heard Hab's voice. "He'm coming directly. He got to go down that mine to get to his demons. When he turn up we'll have the runt, like a rat in a trap."

He didn't know what to do. Without making a sound he moved closer, still keeping himself hidden. Then, as quietly as he could, he picked up a handful of stones.

Holding his breath, he hurled them across the yard – and straight away Hab leapt up.

"He be over there," he hissed.

All three men ran across to where the stones had fallen. After that everything happened at once.

He made a dash for the pithead, clambering onto the first rungs of the ladder. But Hab had seen him. Joel heard him yell, "You leave he to me. I'll catch the runt."

As fast as he could, he climbed down, although he could hear lumbering footsteps just above him.

Passing the first level, he leapt from ladder to ladder, but when he reached the second level he felt Hab's steps getting closer.

His brother was a faster runner. He had longer legs.

In desperation he grabbed for his torch, turning, switching it on, shining it into Hab's face, while Hab threw his hands to his eyes.

Joel didn't let the beam waver though. Aiming it directly, he moved forward, hearing his brother yell, "You brat… You… Devil's child… You..."

Still he advanced, and all the time Hab was staggering towards the shaft, his face twisted with fury…

Then the face began to lose its substance, fading like a reflection in water, until Joel couldn't see it any more.

Instead the torch-beam lit the rock-strewn floor of the rising stope.

Chapter 25

Last week's warmth had gone. This evening the sky was fractured with clouds, driven in on a cold wind. With the unfamiliarity gripping him, he made his way towards Polgwenvor – then along the raised walkway, past Dr Greaves's surgery, past the apothecary's and Burger King. He avoided the glances of passers-by, urgently driving himself until, at last, he reached the turning into Cass's road.

A flood of light shone to the east of Carn Brae, as if the hill was on fire, making him rush towards it. Then he stopped.

Crowds had gathered. The buildings around the mine were hung with coloured lights. On a raised platform Mr and Mrs Blake stood with a group of people. A lady wearing a heavy gold chain was talking into something on a long pole. Her voice sounded odd, enlarged and unnatural, carrying in a hollow echo around the hills.

"Ladies and gentlemen," she was saying. "It gives me great pleasure to declare Wheal Gwenvor open and to re-activate this magnificent engine, the work of our very own local boy, Richard Trevithick."

People began to clap as she turned a sort of wheel, while the gleaming engine standing in front of her burst into motion, setting pistons, levers and cogs working – And – Joel knew, down in the mine, the man-engine and the pumps would be shaking the earth.

In desperation he pushed through, shouting, "No! You can't start that engine."

But people were grabbing at him, holding him back.

"Mr Blake," he called. "Don't. I just got here. It be me, Joel."

He saw Mr Blake steer the lady with the chain to one side. Then he heard him speak. “Is that you, Joel?” His voice rang hollow and unreal around the grounds.

“Yes,” Joel shouted. “You can’t let that engine run. It be dangerous.”

“Let him come up,” said Mr Blake.

Slowly the crowd released him, steering him towards the stage, but the brilliance of the lights swamped him. For a moment he couldn’t see. “I got pictures,” he said at last. “I drawed the old level on the map what you gived me.” He showed Mr Blake. “Up by where you dug that cut the old level do run close. It go right by the roof of the cut. If it crack, the water’s coming in.”

The dignitaries, Mrs Blake, and the lady with the chain were crowding around. But Mr Blake didn’t hesitate. He went straight across to the talking device. “Ladies and Gentlemen,” he said. “There’s been a bit of a hitch. We’ve got to de-activate the engine so we can see what’s going on.” Then he turned the wheel, while the gleaming machine shuddered to a halt.

“Maybe it be too late,” Joel said. “Have you got people down there?”

“Drama students and guides mainly,” said Mr Blake.

By now Cass and Karl were on the stage. “What kept you?” Cass whispered. “We thought you’d be here ages ago.”

“I couldn’t get down to the mine,” he told them. But, if there were people trapped… He’d seen men die in his own time. He mustn’t let it happen again.

“We got to get them out,” he said.

“Sure,” said Mr Blake. “We can’t take chances. If what you’re saying is right and there’s a breach, the lift’s going to pack up. I’ll have to go down – supervise people onto the ladders.”

“I should be there too,” he said. “If something happen, I know that shaft where the ladders is. I been climbing that since I were twelve.”

Cass and Karl wanted to come as well, but Mr Blake shook his head. He suggested they go to the old shaft where the emergency exit came out. “We’ll send a couple into the first two levels to evacuate people there,” he said. “It’s the third level – that’s where the greatest danger is.”

There were people scurrying everywhere. Some of Mr Blake’s assistants headed with him to the lift, stopping off at the first two levels. This time Joel accepted the falling motion. There was no time for fear. One of the assistants stayed, as they went further.

By the time they reached the third level the guides and actors were already gathered in a group. All around the air was hot, with the lozenge lights casting a forlorn glow. Now though, everything had changed. The level was filled with unearthly noises. There were pick-axes and hammers, the chink of metal against rock. It confused him.

“That’s sound effects,” Mr Blake said. “I put them in to get a bit of authentic atmosphere.”

But, to Joel, it felt more like the spirits of the thousands who had sweated and toiled in the mine over the centuries, restless, invisible, working in an eternal hell. He turned to the dip, stumbling towards the cut… And immediately he could see things weren’t right. Puddles had formed on the floor. When he looked up he saw a split in the cut’s roof, spreading like a wound. He knew, soon, the roof would tear itself open. The glass in front of the display would shatter – and the vision he’d seen with the hare and the dog would become a horrible reality.

Mr Blake saw the breach too. Straight away they began shepherding the line of actors towards the emergency exit, but then... A sharp crack – the sound of tumbling water. Glass splintered. The lozenge lights began to flicker. In one eerie moment the whole place turned to darkness, while the disembodied sounds of a working mine gave way to the shattering noise of plunging water, the crash of falling debris and tumbling artefacts.

All around him Joel could feel bodies groping, shoving.

Immediately he took his torch. Already the floor was showing signs of water. "I want to do the leading, sir," he said, pushing through to Mr Blake. "I do know the workings of this mine."

Both Mr Blake and his assistant had torches, while the guides and drama students used tiny lights in their talking devices, but the water from the cut was coming in fast. Now it was well over Joel's ankles. One of the men shouted, "Get a shift on. I've got water up to my knees back here."

By now Joel was pushing on with an urgency, but walking had turned into wading, impeding their progress. Bodies tumbled in disarray behind him.

Then a girl, struggling through the rising flood, made a grab at his shoulder. She was fighting for breath. In his torchlight he could see her face, waxy with perspiration. She was staggering as if she was about to faint. "It's my Asthma," she gasped.

He had no idea what Asthma was, nor did he have any idea what to do, but Mr Blake was beside her.

The others were still desperate. They were barging to get past, and Joel knew that was wrong. It may be this girl was dying. She had to go first.

"Hold still," he shouted. "This here maid be sick. We got to get she to the shaft. The rest of you will be all right. You don't have to shove. We'm nearly there. We'm going to get you out, safe."

Mr Blake called, "Have any of you guys got an inhaler?"

One of the men raised an arm, holding up a small blue cylinder. To Joel's relief, when the girl put it to her lips, the gasping breathlessness eased. "We got to get her out," Mr Blake murmured. "I'll need to support her up the ladders."

By now progress was like walking through treacle. Soon the floods would be up to their thighs.

At last, though, the light from Joel's torch reflected on the safety wall.

"You go up with the maid," he said. "I'll stay back – see them others through."

With Mr Blake and the girl on the ladder, he tried guiding people. Some were less confident. But those behind were still clustering, pushing, desperate to get out. The water was reaching to their mid-riffs now. He knew if he didn't control the pushing no-one would get out.

"Don't you go shoving like that," he shouted. "I got to choose who do go first. Going on like that, none of you is going to get out."

He and Mr Blake's assistant were aiming to let the women through, but one of the young students at the back suddenly panicked. He started pushing at the others, fighting to get to the front. When another student tried to stop him, he hit out. Joel had no idea what to do. These people were older than him, probably stronger. The boy threw more punches. Others joined in. No-one was moving towards the exit. "You got to stop this," he shouted.

At that moment Mr Blake's assistant pushed back to restrain the young man. Then, slowly, as the water crept higher, the number of people dwindled, until it was just Joel, the assistant and the panicking boy. By now the boy was in tears. Joel felt for him. They were so near dying. He could understand his desperation. "It be all right," he said. "You'm scared, that's all. We'm all scared. There ain't no shame in that." He lay his hand on the boy's shoulder and felt him relax. Then, gently he led him towards the shaft.

As they climbed, as a final act, he shone his torch back onto the surging floods – and it was all there – the floating wax boys of his vision, the debris and detritus. He stared for a moment, then shut the emergency door and followed as they clambered towards grass.

He knew, when they reached the shaft's entrance, that this was his pithead – where the engine house and stack, the stamping ground, the vanning troughs of his own time should have been; the dressing floor – the buildings he'd hidden behind only a few hours earlier. But, as he stared around, all he could see was desolation, a vision of decay and age-old destruction.

And this wasn't like the disaster in his time. Blinding flashes stunned him. A small white van with a blue, flashing light stood in a corner. There was a group of men and women gathered around it, checking over the actors, giving them thin fabric sheets to wrap around themselves. The girl who'd been taken ill was there, but there were no bodies on boards, no despair or grief, only people who'd been rescued, anxious to tell their stories. The crowds didn't seem to be there to help either. Instead he saw cameras and other strange devices – with more excitement than grief.

Someone was carrying a device aimed at a young woman. The woman was talking to it, while others crowded around Mr Blake.

Eventually Cass pushed through. When she saw Joel, she ran, putting an arm around him. "You were right," she said. "It happened just like you said. But they're safe – all those guys who were down there."

She pointed to the grey device. "That's television. It's a huge story. It'll be all over the country."

Joel had no idea what 'television' was, but, to him, the group she pointed at – and those talking to Mr Blake – were some kind of rabble, like scrapping magpies. They shouted questions, waving small objects which they pushed into Mr Blake's face, while the lights of cameras flashed all around.

Mr Blake didn't seem to mind.

Cass said it was the press, and he could see why. They were pressing in on her father without any thought for his safety.

Then Mr Blake beckoned him. "It seems you're the talk of the town, Joel," he said, smiling. "This lot want to ask you a few questions. You don't mind, do you?"

Joel still had no idea what was happening. "They seem a bit rough," he said, "I don't know what I got to say to them."

"It's only newspapers and television," said Mr Blake. "Nothing to worry about. If they ask you something tricky, I'll take over. It's best you don't mention where you come from though. I spun this yarn that you're at school still. Tell them you're studying engineering – say you've been sanctioned to use the library at the School of Mines."

"But I don't know nothing about that," he said.

"I know, but what's the alternative? Say you came through a time warp and they'll be on you like a pack of wolves. I said you've got a part time job with me – that you found an old map. The story is, you were scared starting the pumps and man-engine might cause a breach. If you say you came haring over to stop us switching on the Trevithick engine – you can tell them what happened down the mine just as it happened, and don't worry – if they put you on the spot, I'll do the talking."

"You'll be OK," Cass whispered. "Dad's great at dealing with the press."

Mr Blake was already speaking to the girl who had the box trained on her. "OK," he said. "This is the young lad I said about, Joel Penberthy."

One of the press shouted, "Joel?" But Mr Blake held up his hand.

"He isn't the most chatty of individuals. Ask questions to me if you don't mind. I'll pass them over when he's good and ready."

"Was Joel part of the rescue party?" someone shouted.

Mr Blake turned to him. "Do you want to say what happened down there?"

Cass was pushing him. "Go on, Joel. They won't eat you."

He cleared his throat, but he had memories of standing on a chair in the ale house. "I know that mine," he said. "I thought, if it got dark down there, they actors – they ain't used to it – they'd be scared. But I knowed the way good enough. I could lead them out, up the ladder. I knowed where the breach would happen. I knowed where to look."

"Brilliant. You're doing great." Cass whispered.

There were other questions. Some Joel answered, while, with others, Mr Blake stepped in. "You'll be plastered all over the papers tomorrow," Cass's father whispered. "I tell you what, Joel, you'll be the talk of every pub in the land."

Then it was over. The crowds drifted away, the Blakes took Joel and Karl back to their house, and suddenly Joel felt very flat – as if the wind had ceased to blow in his sails. Cass was sitting with him on the settee.

"I'm proper sorry, Mr Blake, sir," he said.

Mr Blake looked at him. "Now, what have you got to be sorry for?" he asked.

"I never stopped it. I knowed what was going to happen, but I never got here soon enough. Now there be that flood – all they wax things floating about."

"Look, son," Mr Blake admitted, "I'm a bit gutted about what happened, I can't deny that; but you did a hero's work. I mean, you saved a good twenty lives here tonight. You got all those people out, and you shut the emergency door before the flood could spread."

"But if I got here as soon as I knowed, I could have stopped it happening. Now your mine – it got ruined."

"Well, if you look at it like that," said Mr Blake, "it's thrown us back a bit, but we've got pumps strong enough to clear the floods, and we can get divers and engineers down to seal the breaches. By the time July and August come, we'll be up and running."

"It'll take so much money though," Joel said.

Cass laughed. "You just don't get the twenty-first century do you, Joel? Dad's insured up to his eyeballs. He paid big money so, if something like this happened, the insurance people would cough up."

But Joel couldn't see it. He'd let everyone down – after they'd done so much for him.

There was coffee and cakes. Mrs Blake and Karl brought them through. "See if there's anything on the news, Alistair," she said.

Mr Blake took a small object lying on the table, and pressed it. Suddenly the black picture frame Joel had noticed over the mantel burst into life – not with a single picture, but with people moving and talking. It was as if he was looking into another world – scenes from places that weren't in the room or even just outside. Then… a mass of faces up by the old shaft. Mr Blake was there, talking just as he'd done an hour earlier – Not only that, but he could see himself. He could hear his own words as if he was saying them all over again.

"How did you do that?" he gasped.

"It's the news," Cass said. "People will be watching this all over the country."

It was like a dream.

"See," she added. "You don't have to be sorry. This will be on TV all night and all day tomorrow. It'll be in every newspaper." She squeezed his waist gently. "You're everybody's hero, Joel Penberthy, but you're more than a hero to us, isn't that right, Dad?"

Mr Blake pressed the little gadget again so that the frame over the mantel went back to its blackened sleep.

"Sure," he said. He smiled, putting a hand on Joel's arm. "And give a thought to all those people who would have been drowned if it wasn't for you, Joel. There'll be a lot of folk around tonight – including us – who'll be thanking you for the rest of their lives."

But there was still something flat inside Joel as they drove to Tehidy.

A squall shuddered over the hill and it seemed that, even in this paradise, grim realities filtered through.

Lives were threatened – the girl who'd been taken ill; the boy who'd panicked. On the camp-site spaces had been left – abandoned by holiday makers returning to daily life.

Yet, in his own time the future was even bleaker. He was terrified as to what his brother would make of the things he'd witnessed down the pit.

"Don't go back," Cass whispered. They were climbing the hill. There was that soft, heart-shaped face under her boyish haircut – the slim figure, and… her dark eyes were pleading.

He'd said goodbye to Karl in the car park. Now it was just the two of them. "Part of me do want to stay," he said. "But this ain't where I belong."

They were standing by the stope, surrounded by bracken, with the flowering gorse and the white-laced May. Cass was crying, and so was he. Life seemed cruel. He so desperately wanted to remain here, but there was his mother and father, Billy Jewell, the Cap'n. Going back was his only choice.

Chapter 26

He expected Hab's mob to be waiting for him in the mine. But when he made it to grass, there was nothing – although that carried its own menace.

Where were they? Why weren't they watching for him?

He'd left potions with his mother, so he made his way straight to the captain's, hiding behind hedges and trees, keeping clear of ale houses and dram shops.

There was a light in Captain Bolitho's window. As soon as the maid opened the door, though, he knew something was wrong. When she saw him, she threw her hands to her face, stepping away. Captain Bolitho pushed at her, telling her to go back to the kitchen. Then he hustled Joel into the drawing room, shutting the front door with an urgency that scared him.

"There've been some funny business going on, Joel, boy," he said.

Joel was almost afraid of what he was going to hear. "What business, Cap'm?" he said.

"A warrant," said the captain, "– and a bounty put on your head. It be Hab and that Sam Eustice – they'm spreading fanciful stories. Now it's the magistrates what want to question you."

Anne Bolitho was standing by the settle. "Word is," she said, "Hab chased you down the pit tonight. He been telling there was a light down there, like the white fires. He'm saying he saw it disappear along with you – into the rock. There wasn't no trace of you. He've gone to the magistrate saying you sold yourself over. He'm saying you'm the devil incarnate. The Pellar, she do say the same."

“I seen what you done for your father, Joel,” Captain Bolitho said. “I can’t see it got nothing to do with no devil, but this tale what Hab be putting about – that don’t seem right.”

Joel didn’t know what to say. To be accused of actually *being* the devil... And with a bounty on his head, there’d be no hiding. He knew he’d have to tell the captain the whole story. If the captain started believing what Hab was saying, he’d have no hope.

“What Hab be saying,” he confessed, “He’m telling the truth, Cap’m.”

Anne Bolitho gasped.

“But, like you saw with Father, it don’t have nothing to do with no devil.”

“This bright light, though, and you disappearing through a solid rock face?” said the captain…

Beginning with the torch in the mine, he told them his story, showing them the things Dr Greaves and Mr Blake had given him, but, while the captain listened, his face remained unchanged.

“What do you think, Anne?” he asked when Joel had finished.

Anne Bolitho didn’t hesitate. “I believe the boy,” she said. “With them instruments and the pictures he’ve showed us, how could I not believe him. And you said yourself, Walter, there ain’t nothing of the devil in what he’m doing for his father.”

“There ain’t,” the captain said. “The care he’ve given to Amos and them potions, they all fit with what he’ve said – and tonight – saving them people’s lives in a future time...” He looked at Joel. “You’m a good boy, Joel. They things what you just told us is amazing, and I know you wouldn’t lie about such things, although...” He shook his head, and Joel could see his face, deeply trouble, "what magistrate, or jury if it come to that, is going to believe a word of it? The summons is out there, boy. If you'm ever to be free in this world you got to answer to the magistrates, and by God, they'll hang you, as sure as day do follow night."

To hear the captain say it in such bald words made Joel's head swim; "What can I do, Cap'm?" he whispered.

The captain was looking hard into the fire's dying embers. "It be late," he said at last. "But night be the best time for this." He moved towards the door. "We'm going over to your father's, boy. We got to tell him and Mother how things stand, and we got to decide, your father and me, because I ain't standing by to see a boy like you hang for saving his father's life."

"What have you got in mind?" his wife asked.

The captain shuffled into his greatcoat. "There'm a way, Anne. I can't say no more, not till I talked it over with Amos and Sarah, but there'm a way."

"Well, you be careful," she said. "The law may be against you, Walter. You remember that."

"That be why it got to be settled now, tonight, before the morning hounds are let loose," he said.

Everything was in darkness at his parents' cottage.

When the captain knocked, there was a flurry of sound along with his mother's voice, and a flickering taper.

"It be Cap'm Bolitho, ma'am," he called. "I'd be obliged if you'd open up. I got urgent need to talk to you and Amos."

The bolt shot, and his mother peered out. "You got Joel?" she said.

Father was lying on the bed. When he saw the captain, he sat up. "Cap'm Bolitho, sir?" he said. He eased himself out, reaching for his crutch, while Joel's mother poked the fire. She put on fresh peats.

"Amos, Sarah," the captain said, finding a seat. "I got to tell you; tonight there've been a bounty put on your Joel. Hab, your other son, be telling how he chased Joel down the mine. He'm telling how he saw him disappear through a solid wall of rock. He've been to the magistrate."

"You know about the wall, Cap'm?" Joel's mother said.

"The boy told me everything, and I don't believe it got nothing to do with the black arts. It be a miracle. In my judgement, Amos, it's thanks to Joel you'm still here." But he went on: "Trouble is, ma'am, with this bounty on him, what with the warrant going out, he've got to face the magistrates. And I don't think, for one minute, they'll believe a word what he do say. If he have to confront a magistrate, it be my belief, he'll hang."

The colour drained from his mother's face. "My Lord," she gasped.

But Joel's father didn't stir. "That ain't going to happen, though, is it, Cap'm?"

"Not if I can help it, Amos," said the captain.

For Joel, everything was going on in a dreamlike unreality. He heard the captain say, "But you, Amos, and Sarah, ma'am, you got to let him go. The boy will only be safe if he get into that future time again. He'll have to live his life out there. I know what a big thing that is, 'specially for you, ma'am. But, if he stay here, you'll lose him to the gallows."

His mother's voice was trembling. "It be hard, Cap'm. I do love that boy with my whole soul."

"All the same, he've got to go. He'll have a better life there. If he stay here he won't have no life at all."

"There ain't no question, Cap'm," Joel's father said. "Do you believe they'll take you, son?"

What Joel was hearing tore at the roots of every emotion. "My friends have begged me to stay, Father," he said. "But I don't know how the doctor nor Mr and Mrs Blake do feel…" He tailed off, looking at his mother – then at his dear father, whose life he'd fought for. "They potions though. What will happen about them if I ain't here?"

"You leave they with me," his mother said. She got up with a sudden determination. "You'm going, boy. And you got a long and happy life in front of you. I won't never see you again. I know that. But you'll be here, all my life – in my head. And in that other place you'll be happy. You'll do well for yourself, because you got brains. I've always said so. You won't never forget your mother nor your father neither. I know that, too."

He realised it was the only way. But his eyes were stinging.

He watched his mother cross to the table so she could brew tea. Doing something with her hands was her only way of dealing with deep feelings. "What will happen now, Cap'm?" she said.

"I'll take the boy down the pit," said the captain. "If it be God's will, he'll find that stope again and he'll be gone. It be best that way, Amos. At least the boy will have a life. They people, they'm good people. You can be certain they'll see he'm all right."

But it was agony – everything he did; explaining how his mother must wash the wound with the salt water, having to hand over the remaining potions, insisting she give Father three pellets every day. He had to say goodbye to those dear people who'd loved him since birth. He had to step out into the cold of the moors and the black night… close the door on his father and mother and Obadiah – be torn from everything he'd grown up to know and love – and he couldn't see how he was going to bear it.

The captain led him back to the mine, although every step away from the cottage and down the shaft brought a stronger pain.

There was Billy Jewel too, and Mary – he would never see them again, nor the captain here.

"If I do find that portal, Cap'm," he said. "There won't be no goodbye nor 'thank you' for what you done. With the stope I don't never know if it be there till I'm in it and I'm climbing to grass – so, what will happen, Cap'm, is this; we'll be walking like we are now, and suddenly I do fade into the rock. I won't be there no more."

"I know that, boy," the captain said. "And when it happen, I'll be witnessing things the like of which I never witnessed before. I'll remember them, too, and you, Joel, till the day I die, and that's a promise."

"I won't never forget you neither, Cap'm," he said. "If I stayed in this world, I would do all I could to make you proud of me. I'd fight my way up to be like you, and I thank you with all I got for how you looked after me."

But, as he was talking, there was a deadening of his voice. His feet were stumbling over a rock-strewn, rising path...

And the captain wasn't there any more.

Chapter 27

There weren't any of the familiar feelings when he reached grass. He was alone on the hill, with the wind gusting. A sliver of moon chased clouds towards the horizon, while areas of an unearthly glow hung over Redruth and Camborne. Every now and then he saw the lights of cars and lorries, like searching rays. Some of the houses in Polgwenvor were in darkness, but others had windows carved out with light.

He found his way down the hill, although his journey was a turmoil of emotions. More cars and lorries trundled past. Small groups of people stood by the road, around bus stands and under the lights illuminating the street. Others wandered aimlessly along the path.

Dr Greaves's house was in darkness. He'd already decided it had to be Dr Greaves and Karl he'd go to. They were nearest, and he felt he knew the doctor better than Mr Blake. But until now he'd only been in the surgery. It took all his courage to strike the door knocker of the main house. The sound echoing around the building made him shudder. Then he saw a light in one of the upstairs windows. Another shone on the glass of the front door. Finally the door opened – the smallest crack; while the doctor's voice said, "Who's there?"

"It be me, sir – Joel," he whispered. The words were choked. "They put a bounty on me in my time. I had to get away. I do need help. I haven't got nowhere to go."

Straight away Dr Greaves pulled the door wide, calling up the stairs. "Helen, Karl, I've got Joel here."

He steered him into a room to the left of the hall. There was a soft warmth to it. Somehow it gave him comfort.

Karl came in, throwing himself into a chair. "What's he doing back here?" he demanded. "Is he in trouble or something?"

"Wait till Mum comes down," said Dr Greaves.

"Are you staying this time, Joel?" Karl asked.

A lady came through. She was dark haired, older looking than Cass's mother, with hair swept across her forehead. It hung to her shoulders. Joel noticed her eyes, the colour of hazel. They glinted warmly.

As she led him to the settee, Dr Greaves perched on the arm of a chair and said, "There's some sort of trouble back in Joel's time. Apparently they've put a bounty on him."

"They are such morons," hissed Karl. "It's because he's using your medicines to cure his dad. What a load of cretins."

"Is that right, Joel?" asked Dr Greaves.

Joel nodded. "Yes, sir, but it be worse. They been hunting me down for all sorts of things. Cap'm Bolitho say I would only stay alive if I was to come here. Back there, he said, they'm going to hang me."

"That's dreadful" said Mrs Greaves. She glanced at her husband. "What can we do, Phil?"

"Well," Dr Greaves said. "We need a conflab with Alistair and Megan for a start."

"And there'll be hell to pay if you don't get Cass over," Karl added.

"Really?" the doctor said, with a half-smile.

He took a small object from the dresser – a bit like the one Cass used when she spoke to her father. "Karl, put some coffee on," he said. "It's late. We need the caffeine."

It wasn't long before he was talking to Mr Blake.

Cass rushed to where Joel was sitting as soon as the Blakes arrived. "Dad told us there's bother," she said.

While he explained, he noticed Karl getting restless again.

He was near to exploding. "Did we really evolve from that bunch of bigots, Dad?" he demanded.

Dr Greaves smiled. "'Fraid so, kid. We've come on a bit, but there's still plenty of that around. Think of what goes on with 'trolls' on the internet – and all the hate crime. We're not that different."

"Yes, but hanging a kid for curing his father. That isn't the sort of place he should be," said Mr Blake.

"What can I do, though," Joel said. "I haven't got no home nor family. I don't belong here."

As soon as he'd said it, Mrs Greaves was by his side, with her arm around his shoulder. "Don't think that, Joel, dear," she said. "You do have a home, either with us or with Alistair and Megan. That's what we're doing, deciding what's best for you."

For a moment it was like hot springs. He couldn't speak.

"Perhaps he should stay with us," Dr Greaves said. He looked at Cass and winked. "What with Joel being such a good-looking guy – and Cass… well… need I say more? It's best they don't live under the same roof, don't you think?"

The colour rose in Cass's face. "Lay off, Phil," she said. "You can be so embarrassing, sometimes."

But Mr Blake was laughing. "Well, that settles it. If there's any chance he'll be messing with our Cass, he's staying with you, Phil."

That made Cass swing around, glaring at her father. "That is really horrible, Dad," she said.

"But, joking apart, Joel," he added. "We owe you such a lot. I mean, you risked your neck coming here earlier. You saved us from something that could have really hit me and Megan. If Phil and Helen do take you on, we want to give a hand – not that Phil needs it. I mean, the guy's a doctor. They aren't paid peanuts. It's just, we would want to be part of your growing up and stuff."

"I could give him home tuition," Mrs Greaves said. "I could get him to some sort of standard where he could start school."

Everything was overwhelming him – running wild in his head.

"There'll be legal issues," said Dr Greaves. "He won't have any papers – no birth certificate or anything – and no way are the authorities going to accept he's a fugitive from the eighteenth century."

"Try Ewan's father, Dad," Karl said. "It's like, he's in the Home Office. He does stuff with immigrants."

There was some comfort in what Joel was hearing, but there was still the pain – the thought of his parents and Obadiah. He knew though... from the moment he'd had that vision, from the moment he'd seen the white hare running with the black dog, his world had been turned upside down. This was his only chance – the only place he'd be safe from the rope and the drop.

The next few weeks were packed with new experiences.

He was in awe of Cass and Karl as they drifted through their daily routines. There were devices they used – Phones, tablets, laptops. They did emailing and texting, surfing the net – things that were a complete mystery to him. Then there were gadgets for preparing food: liquidisers, micro-waves, toasters, coffee makers, ovens that took no visible fuel, fridges, freezers that were constantly colder than the coldest winter night, where food came out in solid blocks, and where nothing ever rotted or grew mouldy.

He went shopping in Truro for new clothes. He'd been to Truro before, but it had changed so much. There was a huge cathedral now that never existed in his time. People thronged through shop-filled streets and precincts. The shops were brightly lit, packed with amazing goods.

Cass insisted they did their shopping on a Saturday, so she could help choose. She informed her mum and Mrs Greaves they were so yesterday's people they wouldn't have a clue about clothes for the modern guy.

He loved his clothes. He loved wearing them. He loved the thought of being like Karl and Ewan.

They visited other types of shops, hypermarkets, where there were so many products – fruits and vegetables that came from every corner of the world. There were packets and boxes, food in freezers, wine in bottles, beers, whisky, brandy, things so exotic he had to be dragged from the displays.

Cass spent a lot of time at the Greaves's house.

She and Karl studied for school. They searched out information on tablets and wrote long pieces on their laptops. Their knowledge of number – the sort of calculations they did – left him speechless.

He was learning too, with Mrs Greaves – Geography, the history of people and events. But not all he learned pleased him. He was dismayed at the machines people had developed to kill and destroy. It wasn't just fighting men they killed either. What they'd invented was used to kill the innocent, the old, women and children, and when he learned about the massacre of two World Wars, he could hardly accept that it had happened.

Mrs Greaves gave him books to read – stories– written through the ages – Dickens, Austen, Hardy – so many. Each book wove its own tale, creating worlds in his head, giving him the chance to live in the souls of other people.

He read eagerly, books where words created pictures and feelings that stayed with him long after he'd reached the final page.

He forgot what it was to be hungry. Each new eating experience was prefaced with Karl and Cass telling him about the food, then watching with delight as he devoured it.

He seemed to be growing closer to Cass. She curled up against him when they were watching television. They went for walks, sometimes with the strange dog, Shelly – roaming the downs and cliffs.

He was intrigued to watch the progress in repairing the mine.

… And he was changing. More and more he was thinking like a twenty-first century boy. He was accepting new things with less confusion.

Karl and Cass contacted Ewan. They talked to him using programs called Snap-Chat and Instagram. When Joel looked, he could see Ewan on their screens, while Ewan said he could see him, Joel Penberthy – even though Joel was in Cornwall and Ewan was in London.

Dr Greaves spoke with Ewan's father. Then, one weekend, Karl and the doctor took him to London.

The train journey was the most amazing thing – huge coaches, a whole snake of them, being pulled by massive engines on steel tracks; through miles of fields, woods and hills; over rivers and roads, through towns that passed in the blink of an eye – and the nearer they got to London the faster the train seemed to go. Karl said that, at one point, they were travelling, covering two miles every minute.

But he didn't like London.

Everything was too much – too many people – too much noise, snarling buses, screams from sirens, and a land crowded with buildings.

Their train took them into a station called Paddington. Karl explained they were in 'rush hour', although he could see that for himself. Everyone was racing around, all with unsmiling faces, pushing to get onto trains and buses, waving taxis down, barging past, showing no manners, ignoring everyone's interests except their own, while mostly, as they shouldered through, they talked on their phones.

The following day they set out to join Ewan and his father. They were going to a place called The Barbican – and... Ewan was there, waiting for them.

Something about the Barbican was different – huge halls and stairways. There were chairs and seats, bars to get food, a place in all the turbulence that gave him some kind of tranquillity.

The boys managed to re-live the whole of the Spring holiday.

Because they'd been on Snap-Chat, Ewan already knew everything about Joel and his escape from his own time. Together they planned for the summer – while Mr Anderson and Dr Greaves worked out how they could make Joel a citizen of their century. It took all Mr Anderson' skills, with no record of him in the twenty-first century. But, as he said, Joel existed. It needed documents to support that. It had to be done.

The only records they discovered were in a log related to Gwenvor mine in the late eighteenth century. There they found a son of Amos and Sarah Penberthy, the second of three boys – an apprentice in the mine. But, according to the mine's log, at the age of fifteen, this Joel had disappeared.

Then, one morning, after he'd been with the Greaves for about five weeks, Dr Greaves brought up a subject that rocked him. "I've been thinking, Joel," he said. "Back in your own time your father will be fully recovered. He'll still have that cast on his leg though."

What Dr Greaves was hinting almost made him choke on his toast. He hadn't forgotten his family, but he was beginning to accept he'd never see them again. "You want for me to go back?" he said.

"Not so much that. It would be too dangerous," the doctor said. "It's just, I guess your father's going to be lumbered with that cast for the rest of his life."

Mrs Greaves looked at her husband, alarmed. "For goodness' sake, Phil, don't go putting ideas into his head. There's still a bounty on him, don't forget. They'll find some way of getting the cast off."

But what Dr Greaves had said brought his parents to the front of his mind, and... he wanted to see them again. He wanted to hear their voices. He wanted to see his dear brother, Obadiah. He knew it would be dangerous, and he wasn't confident he still had the mettle to face the dark moorlands or the scrub-strewn wastes. He would be dragged to the magistrates if he was found. But – to get the cast off, to complete what he'd started, to watch his dear father walk again... "I got to go, Mrs Greaves," he said. "If I went towards evening there wouldn't be nobody about. They ain't going to be looking out for me, not like they was when I come here."

Karl thought the idea was crazy, and Cass was emphatic he shouldn't go. "If you go and you don't come back," she said, "I'll die."

"But I will come back," he insisted. He wasn't prepared to let any other possibility enter his head.

"Well, if you go," she repeated, "I'll wait up by the stope, and if you don't come back, I'll just stay there till I'm dead."

There was no shifting him though.

Two days later they drove to Tehidy car park, climbing the hill one final time. He had his croust bag with a battery powered saw tucked inside. Cass clung to him as they climbed. "I will wait," she said. "Phil and Karl can go home, that's OK, but I won't move, not until you come back out of that stope."

It was the height of summer, although he knew, in his own time, the world would be frozen into the darkness of deepest winter – and now that he was at the mouth of the stope, he was beginning to wonder if this was the right thing to do. His goodbyes were tinged with fear. The stope was taking him towards a place where every crack of a broken twig, every dislodged stone tumbling from a damaged wall, every brush with bracken or gorse could bring about discovery – and that would mean certain death.

All the same, he set out, using a torch to follow through passages, until the ground levelled – and all the smells were there, the age-old stone and earth, the corrupt air, the hint of gunpowder, the stench of chemicals that he now knew were arsenic and the ore of copper and tin. He could hear, again, the scuffling of rats, the groan of timbers.

This time it took an age climbing to grass. He knew he'd lost the fitness that came with labouring in the mine.

There was a silence at the pithead – only disturbed by the soft pumping of the beam engine. He stood for a moment, smelling the sweetness of the oil and the cold sharpness of a biting frost. It was a clear night, with the stars suspended like frozen diamonds in the winter sky. The trek to the cottage seemed longer than he remembered, and every step carried potential hazards. The hedges appeared ghostly, barely visible, the grass crisp. All the time his eyes were searching for movements that might spell danger. In the distance he heard singing from an ale house, but the moors remained deserted. Then, as he pushed through the hedge, there again was the small, white cottage in its field, with the shuddering glow of a taper burning in the window. Immediately his anxiety faded. This was his home. The people in this cottage were his family. Gently he pushed open the door.

His father and mother were sitting by the fire, with Obadiah curled at the back of the room, asleep.

As soon as she saw him, his mother sprang up. She gripped the mantel and her eyes stared. "Is that you, Joel, boy?" she whispered.

He closed the door, stepping further into the room. "I comed back to take the cast off Father's leg," he said.

His mother didn't move. It was as if she was seeing a ghost. Then she rushed across to grab him. "I never thought to see you again," she said. She pulled him towards the fire. "Give us a proper look. They clothes you got on –"

His father turned in his chair, his face glowing with a deep joy. "It be handsome to see you, son," he said.

All the emotions were there again. His mother, his father; Obadiah asleep in his corner. As he looked at them, he realised how much he'd missed them.

"They clothes, all well made and good quality," his mother said. "Whatever tailor sewed them is skilled." She poked him in the midriff. "You'm filling out too. There be more flesh on you."

In a second Obadiah uncurled himself. Then he was across the room, hugging Joel, demanding to know all about his new life. It was hard. Joel loved this boy, but he had to ease himself away.

"It ain't safe, me being here," he said, looking at his father. "I got to do what I comed for. Then I got to go back.

I'm safe back there with the doctor and his wife. They'm like a father and mother to me."

"Don't say it, Joel, boy," his mother whispered. She held up her hand. "It be me what gived birth to you. It do break my heart thinking what our neighbours have done – how your own brother drove you away."

"You'll always be my mother and father and my brother in my soul," he said. "But, you know, just like I do, if I stay, they'm going to hang me."

"It's true, it be for your own good," she said. "But you'm in my thoughts – every day – you have been ever since you went, and you always will be."

The job he came to do, though, it had to be done, and he had to get clear before he was caught. He took the saw from his croust bag.

"Don't you go rushing with that leg, Joel, boy," his mother whispered. "We don't want to part with you again, not so soon."

Obadiah helped him, steadying the leg, while, carefully, he began to cut through the plaster. Then he took the mould, handing it to his younger brother.

With the plaster gone, his father's leg was as straight as it had ever been. The wound was healing to a clean scar. It left Joel with a deep satisfaction. "That leg will be like it always was, Father," he said. "You won't need that crutch no more. It be all right to put your whole weight down now – Dr Greaves said."

His father looked at him. The trust and gratitude were there again – and that ripped through him. In the next minutes he would have to leave these people, his folk, his family. This time he knew it would be forever.

He watched as his father took the first few steps. "It won't come easy to start with," he said. "They muscles be weak. But you ain't going to be lame. You'll be working in that mine, just like you always did."

"I wouldn't never have believed it," his mother said. "Not unless I seen it with my own eyes. You done a wonderful thing, boy."

Leaving was an agony, even though he knew every second he stayed put him in danger.

But he also knew, in a future time, Cass was waiting for him up by the stope. Ahead of him lay a summer with his three friends – and a whole new life. The memory of his father walking though, of his mother standing over the fire, and Obadiah hugging the discarded cast – those images…

Tears blinded him as he stumbled towards the mine. He could hardly make out the hedgerows, or the stretches of fields and moorland.

This time the climb into the pit had that air of finality, although thoughts scared him. If he couldn't find the stope, he'd be caught in this world for ever, under threat of death… and Cass, waiting for him at the pit's entrance… he'd never see her or Karl or Ewan again. He wondered – would she really stay there until she died? But none of it bore thinking about. He had to find the stope and make the journey. He had no other choice, although, as he staggered between pit-props and broken walls, he was still crying for his mother and father, and for Obadiah.

Finally, though, he found himself climbing, struggling with tumbled rocks and landfalls. There was that pale light ahead of him. Soon he was smelling the fresh salt of the sea, the warmth of a July evening. In front of him he could make out the mouth of the shaft and the deep purple of a darkening summer sky.

For a moment he stood, contemplating the future. It was all out there, shrouded with the mysteries of time. But behind him lay a long dark passage to the past, to the family he loved. He was hit with a longing, a yearning pain. He knew he had to take one last look into the stope, to the world of his birth.

After that he would go to Cass and the future.

As he turned, though, to shine his torch deep into the tunnel, he gasped.

… The stope wasn't there any more. The tunnel that he'd struggled through so many times, the tunnel that had taken him to and from his home had disappeared. It was just the wall of broken rock and stone that Dr Greaves had described, piled to the cave's roof.

Stunned, he let the torch shine on, but there was no portal… And slowly a realisation gripped him. From now on he could never go back. His dear family had been shut away from him for ever, by rock falls and the centuries of time.

He felt a bitter sadness.

He would never forget what was back there, his father, his mother, Obadiah, The Cap'm and Billy Jewell – but the blocking of the centuries did something else – something amazing.

Joel Penberthy, son of Amos and Sarah, born into a time long gone, was no longer a child of the eighteenth century. He was, at last, completely and utterly, a twenty-first century boy, anchored in this new, amazing world.

He only had the future to look to.

Reluctantly he turned, taking one last, lingering glance at the blocked stope.

Then he walked towards the mine's mouth, to the warm night, where the sky was cloudless, and where, in the twilight, he could see Cass – his own dear Cass. She'd been sitting on the grassy outcrop all the time he'd been away.

As soon she saw him, she leapt up. Her face lit with that soul-melting smile – and without hesitation, he ran towards her.

europe books